D1477648

THIS series of SCANDINAVIAN CLASSICS is published
by The American-Scandinavian Foundation in the
belief that greater familiarity with the chief literary
monuments of the North will help Americans to a
better understanding of Scandinavians, and thus serve
to stimulate their sympathetic coöperation to good ends

SCANDINAVIAN CLASSICS
VOLUME XII

SARA VIDEBECK
THE CHAPEL
BY
C. J. L. ALMQUIST

SARA VIDEBECK

AND

THE CHAPEL

By C. J. L. ALMQUIST

TRANSLATED FROM THE SWEDISH

BY ADOLPH BURNETT BENSON

Author of "Swedish Romanticism"

NEW YORK

THE AMERICAN-SCANDINAVIAN FOUNDATION

LONDON: HUMPHREY MILFORD

OXFORD UNIVERSITY PRESS

1919

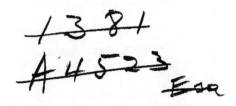

A734483
BH

D. B. Updike · The Merrymount Press · Boston · U.S.A.

CONTENTS

Introduction

THE years 1830 to 1850 formed a period of unrest in Europe. The artistic freedom and individualism of the Romantic revolt had helped to prepare the way for social and political liberalism, while a more intense study of history, folklore, and language had stimulated a greater interest in the common people. Romanticism, vague and subjective, had contained from the first the elements of dissolution. Its late sponsors, therefore, sensitive to both their own poetic self and the more objective trend of the time, vacillated between the unreal and the real, until the latter predominated, giving birth to realism. Obviously, Scandinavia could not remain immune to the strong current tendencies in other countries, a fact which is best exemplified, perhaps, in the work of a Swedish writer, Carl Jonas Love Almquist. Though singularly independent, the strange novelist represents both the culmination and decline of the Romantic cult and the beginning of a new order. His best literary products appeared during this unsettled period of transition, and the two here offered, both pioneers of their kind, and published in the fourth decade, indicate a new democratic, realistic spirit in Northern culture.

Almquist is undoubtedly the most bizarre genius in Swedish letters. Indeed, a modern editor designates him as "the most important and most gifted of Swedish writers at the middle of the last century." The descriptive epithet "a man of contradictions," so often applied to Strindberg, may well be applied to Almquist also. Seldom have so many paradoxes and inconsistencies been combined in the same personality. Deep in his inner life, however, we find a unity of mystical, religious feeling. We find also in his dualistic nature a more or less well-defined unity of purpose, for his diligence, versatility, and productivity show that Almquist believed he was born to reform the existing conventional standards and had a great mission to fulfill in Swedish literature.

Almquist was born in Stockholm, November 28, 1793. Among his paternal ancestors were many prominent Lutheran clergymen. His father bore the title of "military commissary," but was in reality a farmer in Uppland, an unimaginative man of affairs who cared for nothing but figures. His mother, of a distinguished intellectual family, was an introspective, passionate woman, whose "favorite pastime was to wander around in parks and woods, preferably alone or with Rousseau." There had never been any mental or spiritual sympathy between his parents, and much of Almquist's attitude toward marriage must be traced to what he saw in his own home. Thus the impressionable youth was sent out into the world, as he said, with two souls: a poetic soul, the inheritance from his mother, and an "accountant soul," from his father.

Young Almquist spent a part of his time on the farm and a part in his native city. He learned to love outdoor life, studied the landscapes with fervid attention, and acquired a deep aversion for urban conventionalities. Rousseauism never had a more enthusiastic votary. His tendency toward a dreamy religiosity was fostered, after the untimely death of his mother, by his maternal grandfather, the learned Gjörwell, a sympathetic admirer of the Moravians. This early pietistic influence was supplemented later by the study of Swedenborg, who became a favorite guide in Almquist's religious speculations.

Gjörwell soon discovered the potentialities of his grandson, encouraged his desire for many-sided learning, and hoped to make him an historian. Almquist read everything that he could find, prepared for the university, and entered Uppsala in 1808. He took the master's degree, in 1815, with distinction, then served for five years as tutor to a Finnish nobleman. From 1820 to 1824 he was a clerk in the ecclesiastical department in Stockholm.

Meanwhile Almquist had begun to expound his love for the "simple and instinctive," and in 1816 had joined the Manhem Society. This group of enthusiasts, like the members of the older so-called Gothic Society, purposed to emulate the example of their Scandinavian forefathers and live a more vigorous, primitive life, in closer contact with nature. Almquist resolved to get away from the Stockholm atmosphere, and took a bold step. He bought a little farm in Värmland, married a young country girl, called himself "Yeoman Carlsson," and settled down to a "life of antediluvian innocence."

All went well in the beginning; Almquist divided his time between tilling the soil and reading and writing. But soon the literary interests of the idealist eclipsed all practical considerations, and he was obliged to move back to the capital after only two years. He supported himself and his family temporarily by copying, until he was appointed a teacher in the New Elementary School, an institution established for pedagogical experimentation. He became principal in 1829 and was commissioned to write text-books for the various courses. Again, all went well at first, for Almquist was interested in educational problems; but his literary plans soon assumed gigantic proportions. His teaching probably suffered as a consequence, and many complaints of neglect were registered against him. His ordination as a Lutheran pastor did not open any better prospects—the only position he ever held as minister of the Gospel was that of regimental chaplain—nor was he successful in obtaining a coveted professorship in Lund. Embittered by opposition and misunderstanding and prompted by his greater interest in writing as well as by the more definite economic advantages offered by journalism, he broke all bonds and, in 1839, joined the editorial staff of *Aftonbladet*, the organ of the liberalists. Two years later he resigned as principal of the school.

Despite his phenomenal industry and considerable income, Almquist's finances were far from satisfactory, and though he made separate provision for his family, hoping this might improve his affairs, it was evident that they would never be any better. The lack of appreciation of his work and aspirations shown by his peasant wife added to his discontent. The crash came when, in 1851, he made his way secretly through Bremen and London to America, leaving his debts behind, and exposing himself thereby to charges of a still more serious nature.

Almquist's life in the United States was one continuous struggle for existence. He lived in various places, under assumed names, supporting him-

self by writing and by giving lessons in English
and Latin. At one time he is said to have collected
Indian melodies in the vicinity of Niagara. When
the Civil War broke out, Almquist was in New
Orleans and, being an enthusiastic Unionist, an
opponent of slavery, and an admirer of Lincoln,
he found himself obliged to seek refuge elsewhere.
He started for Mexico, but was robbed in Texas,
and had to move north rather precipitately, losing
several manuscripts, which he never recovered. He
took great interest in the progress of the war, but
was too old to shoulder a musket. In 1865, still
engaged in pretentious literary enterprises, he left
America for Bremen. There he died in September
of the following year, at the age of seventy-three.
He was first buried in Bremen, but in 1901 his remains were removed to Sweden.

The writings of Almquist embrace many forms and
subjects, treat of many ages in history, and are local-
ized in many parts of the globe. Ethics, religion,
philosophy, literary criticism and history, agricul-
ture, and social and political problems are treated
by this curious intellect, who was a law unto himself and followed only the dictates of his own convictions and the whims of his boundless fancy.
Even those of his productions that belong more

strictly to polite literature are often filled with scientific, geographical, and linguistic erudition—much of it introduced for effect—or serve as vehicles for his conception of life. Notwithstanding the variety in what came from his pen, Almquist created some real works of art, and despite the broad scope of his interests, his learning has something more than the superficiality of the dilettant.

In a clever, humorous satire, written in 1814, Almquist began to show the underlying tendencies of his nature. Other works from early manhood comprise sagas, legends, and philosophical articles, which glorify natural scenery and a Rousseauan life or advocate a passive relation with God and a closer identification with the Absolute or, as Almquist called it, "the whole." His first important product is *Amorina*, a long, fantastic piece in dramatic form, a Neo-Romantic arabesque, raised to the highest power, with all the ardor and imagery of a youthful poet's imagination, and permeated with all the liberal and esthetic principles of its author. It was ready for the press in 1822, but did not appear until 1839, the same year as *Sara Videbeck*.

Most of Almquist's works were published in a collection of fourteen volumes, called *Törnrosens Bok* (*The Book of the Briar Rose*), which began to appear in 1832. This series was designed to give a complete picture of life, with both thorns and roses, as the name implies, as well as a comprehensive idea of human thought, literature, and knowledge. In the author's mind, the colossal undertaking formed an organic unity and was intended to be a universal work of encyclopedic aim. Almquist worked long and seriously in formulating his plans; many of the productions incorporated in the final series were probably written during the twenties. As long as he lived, he labored to increase the scope of his "book," and when he passed away, some fourteen hundred neatly written folio pages of manuscript were ready to be added to his literary legacy. It grew very rhapsodically, however, and the only inner unity is the unity of authorship. Externally, the separate parts are linked through being narrated to one listener by different members of a fictitious literary coterie representing various phases of the author's self.

A celebrated work from the *Törnros* series is *The Queen's Diamond*, and one of the most fascinating characters in Swedish Romantic literature is the figure of its heroine, Tintomara. Like the heroine of *Amorina*, her actions are motivated by instinct, but it takes a different form. Tintomara is utterly incapable of falling in love, which serves only to intensify her charms, and compels her to

spend a great part of her life in dodging the atten-
tions of the other sex. At times the mysterious,
animal-like maiden dons the garb of a page. The
value of the novel as a whole, besides the poetic
interest in the heroine, lies in the historical setting, centred as it is about the Frenchified court of
Gustavus III, whose murder in 1792 forms the
main pivot of the narrative.

Sara Videbeck (*Det går an*) is historically the
most important of all Almquist's works. A landmark in Swedish fiction, it is probably the most
striking and discussed literary product from the
dawn of realism and feminism in Scandinavia. When
it was first printed, in 1838, the author's friends
besought him not to distribute any more copies,
and the edition was destroyed. It appeared again
the following year, however, this time being provided with an Introduction (here printed as an Epilogue), which made clear the meaning of the story.

As a novel with a "tendency," *Sara Videbeck*
has high technical merit. Karl Warburg is undoubtedly justified in saying that from a purely artistic
standpoint it is "one of Almquist's most finished
productions." By reason of its clear, simple, straightforward narrative, it is "a masterpiece of realistic
description and in this respect holds a unique place
in contemporaneous prose fiction." The impatient

but good-hearted sergeant and especially the attractive, refreshing heroine, a veritable creation in literature, are characters whom we should like to know. Almquist's enthusiasm for the less fortunate classes in general wins our respect and sympathy. The novel contains some very touching, singularly dramatic situations, and is motivated with exceptional force.

Contemporary critics paid more attention to the teachings of the work than to its delightful literary qualities. It called forth protests from many quarters, and Almquist was asked to explain its moral import. Vehement controversies in social and ethical questions resulted, and became a determining factor in the author's later career. But the moralizing contents must be studied against the background of European tendencies. *Sara Videbeck* represents merely one battle in the general campaign of feminism that was carried on during the thirties in France, Germany, and to some extent in England and Scandinavia. The form of marital union proposed by Sara Videbeck, moreover, is highly idealistic in theory and spirit and by no means so radical as many have supposed, being based on rational love, economic independence, and depth and strength of character. Sara is a practical type of woman, whose convictions have been moulded

by external and by no means impossible circumstances. She knows her own mind and heart, makes
her own living, and is wholly capable of taking care
of herself.

Sara Videbeck had a marked influence on Swedish letters with respect to both style and content.
It gave the impulse also for a flood of argumenta-
tive *Sara Videbeck* literature; even unsympathetic
writers appropriated suggestions from its themes
and descriptions. Almquist lacked balance and firm-
ness — only a few stanch friends supported openly
his ideals — and it was not until much later, when
his artistry and social ethics were studied in the
light of evolutionary development, that he found
less reluctant disciples. Modern feminists, however,
have received fruitful impressions from Almquist.
Among them is the moralist Ellen Key, who has
called him "Sweden's most modern writer."

The Chapel (*Kapellet*), Almquist's most pleasing
and beautiful tale of the common people, portrays
an ideal Christian minister, who chooses a congregation of poor fishermen in preference to a more
lucrative parish. It appeared in 1838, the year after
the author's ordination, which may explain much
of the hero's profound sense of religious respon-
sibility. The young pastor's Christianity, however,
assumes a new practical, philanthropic form: the

missionary of God must first be himself a man of *deeds* and sacrifices, and should, above all, begin his work of charity at home. *The Chapel* has long been a Swedish and Danish choice for wholesome folk-reading, and will contribute materially to perpetuate the name of Almquist. Its vivid descriptions and scraggy, weather-beaten, poverty-stricken characters produce an impression that is scarcely paralleled in Swedish fiction. Technically, the story attains the same perfection as *Sara Videbeck*.

Almquist represents a fusion of eighteenth-century feeling, Storm-and-Stress disregard for rules, Fichte-Schelling philosophy, and Swedish Fosforism. He had been impressed by the English novels of terror and supernaturalism, and had found much literary stimulus in Romanticists like Tieck, Novalis, Fouqué, Werner, and Hoffman. Victor Hugo and George Sand — Almquist paid a visit to France in 1840 — appealed strongly to his love of esthetic independence. He was possessed of an extraordinary originality and imagination, and believed in the sovereignty and divine mission of genius. He also shared the interest of his contemporaries in the historical past, but his was a poetic interest, pure and simple; Almquist was no reactionary in a political sense, as so many orthodox Romanticists are.

It is not surprising that we should find the Muse of this writer in polite literature essentially lyrical. He had the poet's sensitiveness to the lyric beauties in life, and even his dramas resemble pictures or tableaux, divided into scenes, with an underlying subjective quality. Yet the quantity of his purely lyric poetry is very small. Nor was Almquist a great lyrist; his best field is in the shorter forms of prose fiction, in which the novel with a tendency is conspicuous. His ability to introduce his moral thesis without detracting seriously from the interest of the narrative is remarkable. In his work the two elements seem mutually necessary and complementary.

As we might expect, Almquist displays great variety in form and style. He tells us himself that he painted as he pleased. In the *Songs*, a small collection of short lyrics in the Fosforistic vein, and in his dramatic poems, he evinces the Romantic fondness for metrical experimentation. Often verse and prose supplement each other in the same work, and are sometimes accompanied by his own improvised music to the songs. His verse, however, is occasionally marred by padding. Almquist was a clear but not always a deep thinker, and he attempts to compensate for his poverty of thought by a skillful jingle of words.

Authorities have differed greatly in their esti-
mates of Almquist as a writer. He did not prove
to be the Messiah of Swedish letters which some
early contemporaries thought him, but the pro-
phecy of his friends that his work would be better
appreciated later has come true. Since 1880 the
star of his native fame has risen considerably, and
modern Swedish historians have devoted a large
proportion of space to him and his influence. In
the well-known anthology of *Sveriges National-
Litteratur*, a whole volume, out of a total of twenty-
six, is given to Almquist — a distinction shared
only by Runeberg and Strindberg — and the late
Karl Warburg, in the *Illustrerad Svensk Litteratur-
Historia*, honors him with over a hundred pages of
biography and criticism. It is now recognized that
Almquist has accomplished much of real value,
especially in introducing the realistic tale of the
common people into Swedish literature.

Almquist is very little known in America. He
has never attained the international fame of some
other Swedish writers, and his direct influence is
limited, for the most part, to northern Continental
Europe. A number of his works have been published in Danish, Finnish, and German, but so far
as the translator has been able to determine, none
of them have been done into other languages. *Sara*

Videbeck and *The Chapel* are his first stories, then, to appear in English.

I beg to acknowledge a debt of gratitude to Professor William Henry Schofield and Dr. Henry Goddard Leach, members of the Publication Committee, and to Miss Hanna Astrup Larsen for all courtesy and editorial assistance. In this maiden effort to reproduce a literary work of my native tongue in English, their suggestions, especially in the matter of form, have been of exceptionally great value. For shortcomings in the translation I alone am responsible.

A. B. B.

SARA VIDEBECK

[*Det går an*]

1839

SARA VIDEBECK

Chapter I

"'A charming and remarkable intermediate! Not a
country girl, not at all a peasant girl—nor yet entirely of the better class.'"

ONE beautiful Thursday morning in July, a
large crowd of people passed Riddarholm
Church and hurried down the hill between
the Exchequer and the Public Treasury, so as not
to be late at the Maelar dock, where the steamboats
lay. All were bound for the *Yngve Frey,* and ran
quickly over the gangplank, for the hour of sailing
had struck, and the captain had commanded "Visitors off deck!"

So the visitors said a brief farewell to their friends
and went ashore. The gangplank was pulled in, and
the steamer started. After a few minutes it was far
out on the water.

"It's no use! It's too late, madam!" exclaimed
a few travelers with half-mischievous eagerness,
when an elderly lady was seen coming down to the
Riddarholm landing, waving her handkerchief, and
indicating by violent gesticulations that she was a
passenger who ought to be aboard. There was no
boat ready near the shore, and the steamer was
shooting like an arrow past the Military Hospital.

Nevertheless, a certain commotion, though brief,

was aroused among the passengers when they heard
half-suppressed cries from a young woman on the
fore-deck: "My aunt! My aunt!" She seemed un-
willing, for the sake of propriety, to call aloud, but
it was evident that she had been separated in an
annoying way from a relative, presumably an expected traveling-companion of some importance to
her.

But we are often so self-absorbed that we forget
our neighbors; and those who purchase tickets for
the saloon or stern do not care particularly what
happens to the rabble on the fore-deck or near the
forecastle. This time the "better" travelers consisted
of elderly gentlemen, almost all of whom had sad
faces. They were accompanied by wives and children, not the very youngest, perhaps, but boys and
girls in that transitional age when naïveté has disappeared, and has not been succeeded by sentiment
and reason. All such people are highly egotistic,
and for obvious reasons. Children of this class are
generally so incapable of taking care of themselves
that they cry for help every moment: now a shoe-
lace has become untied, now a glove has fallen over-
board; now they are hungry, now thirsty; and the
whole world is out of order. Consequently, their
mothers have a great deal of trouble, besides the
care they have to take of themselves in climbing
up and down the narrow stairs of the steamboat.
Finally, the fathers of the families try to cheer up by

taking snuff and reading newspapers; but even this seems insufficient. These passengers cannot devote much attention to others, for they have enough to do in looking out for themselves, their wives, and their children. Above all, they must consider very attentively what they may venture to eat on board without becoming completely bankrupt; for the natural reason that, when the pure joy of the soul, which is the best medicine against disorders and weakness of the body, is gone, one is constantly susceptible, and becomes readily indisposed both from what one does eat and from what one does not. Many gentlemen here still had lingering memories of cholera. No wonder, then, that each one thought of himself and, with a seriousness in his demeanor befitting a Roman senator, considered, pondered, and deliberated, until finally, so far as it was possible, he had decided upon a plan for his food and other important details of the voyage.

If there had been among the saloon passengers a young unmarried man, he would very likely have taken pity on the poor woman on the fore-deck who had been separated from her aunt; at least he would have found out how she looked and what her name was.

This time there was no such man on the *Yngve Frey*. But among the fore-deck passengers was a tall and handsome non-commissioned officer—to be exact, a sergeant—who, on this trip, either for

lack of money or for other reasons, had not cared
to travel better. As he was very agreeable and gen-
tlemanly, he conversed with some of the saloon
passengers. He was not spurned by these, because
his mustache was dark, turned up, and looked almost beautiful; his doublet was neat enough not to
displease the matrons; and a certain manliness in
his bearing permitted the fathers, who otherwise
would have been stately and stiff, to enter into conversation with a person who seemed to convey a
silent promise not to remain a non-commissioned
officer, but in time to become at least a lieutenant
if not a captain or major.

On the fore-deck, the nice young sergeant noticed the girl who had been separated from her
aunt, and it attracted his attention that she had removed the neat little hat of white cambric which
she wore at leaving, and after a while appeared in
a silk kerchief resembling that worn by a maid-
servant. He wondered whether she belonged to that
class, or whether she were not a little higher in the
social scale. And why did she change her head-dress?

The sergeant, who had become interested in her
through her first misfortune, began to confine himself more and more to the fore-deck where he
really belonged, and gradually gave up his conversation with the noblesse of the cabin. "This handsome girl," he said to himself, "appears to me to
belong to the upper middle class — probably from

some country province—and is on her way home,
accompanied and protected by an older relative,
who has been prevented by her cup of coffee from
getting to the steamboat on time. When this happened, the girl wished to avoid the impropriety of
traveling as a young lady without an escort. So she
instantly removed her hat, and by putting on her
kerchief transformed herself into an ordinary girl
like the four or five servant girls on the fore-deck;
and as such she could continue to travel at least
the length of the Maelar without scandal, though
without her aunt."

Whether this was good reasoning or not, the sergeant fixed his attention on the little scene. It was
never clear in his mind whether the girl was really
of the higher or lower class; but at all events she
was neat and tidy in her dark gray capote. The large
kerchief of fine pale pinkish silk with a few narrow green stripes here and there had been tied
under her chin and over the comb in the back of
her hair to form a tasteful head-dress, such as was
formerly called a wimple. This so pleased the sergeant that he never thought of yearning for the
cambric hat. He went down to the captain to inquire who she was. After examining the passenger
list for a moment, he found that her name was Sara
Videbeck, and that she was a glazier's daughter
from Lidköping. An unusually circumstantial bit
of information in a list of steamboat passengers!

It happened to be available because she was provided with a passport, which is seldom the case with steamboat travelers, and because she had had sense enough to leave it with the captain during the journey, so as to obtain the greatest possible security for her person.

The sergeant sat in deep thought down in the dining-hall—mark what I say, dining-hall—where fore-deck passengers might penetrate at mealtime, at least those of sufficient courage and sprightly appearance. It was now about breakfast time, or it could easily become that by ordering a portion of food. The sergeant meditated as follows: "A glazier's daughter from Lidköping—that's a small town far, far from Stockholm. Yes, she is what I took her for—a daughter of the middle class, yet not of the lowest grade. A charming and remarkable intermediate! Not a country girl, not at all a peasant girl—nor yet entirely of the better class. What is the real status of such an individual? How shall I address her? There is something puzzling about this intermediate state. Let me see—Bring me a beefsteak!"

The breakfast made a fitting pause in the sergeant's rambling and confused train of thought. When he had finished the beefsteak, he continued to himself: "The deuce! Upon my word, that's just what I am—in between! What am I, forsooth? I am not a private. Not an officer. I am not of the lower class, and yet nothing really better. Let me see—Oh, the devil—Bring me some porter!"

After he had drunk his porter, the sergeant got up, twisted his mustache, spat far into the left corner of the dining-hall, and paid for his breakfast. "Hm!" he thought, "Sara—Vid—Vid— has had nothing to eat this morning. I have a good mind to go and find out if she can be spoken to or invited—if she, perchance, can eat—" The sergeant's reasoning, now as before, was a bit erratic; it led to no conclusion this time either, and ended in a pause. He inspected his boots, and found them polished; his doublet was brushed and in excellent condition. With two elastic steps the slender young soldier reached the deck, looked about, and centred his attention on the forepart of the ship.

The first he saw there was a crowd of Dalecarlian women standing near a group of the above-mentioned four or five servant girls and a couple of begrimed machinists. A head in pink was there, too. The sergeant approached. He heard the Dalecarlian women offer rings of horsehair for sale— black, white, green, and red—with name and motto artistically inserted. They wanted the girls to buy, but the girls stood firm, and kept bargaining about the price. The sergeant did not hear the one with the pink head-dress bargaining exactly, but he saw her examining the rings with great scrupulousness until, finally, she chose a plain one, black and white,

without any inscription. The woman from Dalecarlia gave the price as threepence. The head in
pink nodded assent, whereupon a little purse—a
bag knit of green silk—was pulled from her capote,
and a silver coin appeared in her hand, lying neatly
on the palm of her lilac-colored glove. The silver
coin was of the smallest Swedish denomination,
sixpence. "Can you give me back three pennies in
change?" said a pleasant voice, with a Västergötland accent of the more agreeable kind and with
a slight harshness of the r. "Three pennies in
change?" remarked the woman from Dalecarlia.
"Ah, my dear girl, I am afraid I haven't got any,
but you might just as well buy two rings from me,
then it will be just sixpence. Buy! Do buy!"

"No, indeed!" was heard from the pretty head.
The sergeant, who stood behind and saw only her
neck, had no other indication that the answer came
from her than that her head was bent forward a
little.

Now the sergeant came forth gaily and said:
"Permit me, Miss Vid—" he checked himself—
"permit me—hm!—to purchase those two rings
from the Dalecarlian woman." He put a sixpence
into the woman's hands, and, without further ceremony, took the two black and white rings, which
the woman held up in the air in the hope of selling
them. The girl in pink looked up at the soldier, a
bit astonished. But he, unembarrassed, immediately

handed her the ring which she had chosen before, and said: " Was it not this one that Miss Sar—hm!—was n't it this very one you wanted? Please take it and keep it! I will keep the other myself."

The girl looked at him with rather pretty eyes, he thought. In truth, amazed as she was, she took the ring he offered her; but when he imagined that she was about to put it on the finger for which she herself had intended it, he noticed that, instead of doing so, she withdrew slowly to the railing and, without saying a word, dropped the ring into the lake.

"Prosit, sergeant!" he said to himself when he saw the move. "That means that I am thoroughly squelched. Bravo, youngster! Why should I call her Miss Videbeck when she has put on a wimple and wants to be unknown? Rather address such a person as Sara at once, if need be. Why offer a ring to a strange girl? And right on deck, too! Shame on you, Albert!"

He went to the railing opposite, took the other horsehair ring, which he had already put on his finger, and threw that too into the lake. At the same time he spat upon the salute gun which lay close by. Then he promenaded down the deck to the stern, and, when he again approached the fore-deck, chance would have it that he should come right in front of the pink stranger, who stood and watched the working of the machinery. "You see," he said, showing his hands, "I too have thrown my ring into the lake. It was the best we could do."

First a sharp survey from top to toe, followed immediately, however, by an almost imperceptible though tolerably sweet smile, then an exquisitely sparkling look, which instantly disappeared, constituted her answer. "Is the ring in the lake? Oh!" she added.

"I hope a pickerel has already swallowed it," said the sergeant.

"A big perch took mine."

"Now when the pickerel swallows the perch," resumed the sergeant, and bowed his head, "which I hope will happen very soon, the two rings will still come to lie — under the same — heart." The last was whispered with a tender protraction of the words, but the sergeant's purpose failed completely. The girl turned away abruptly without answering, and joined the other maids.

"Prosit, my boy!" he said to himself. "Squelched again! And why speak of a heart? And on deck! But one thing pleases me: she did n't take it amiss that I ventured to address her at all. Therefore, don't be faint-hearted!"

He went down into the dining-room and bought a cigar, lighted it, came up again, sat down on his trunk with a free and lofty mien, drew long clouds of smoke from his cigar, and seemed content.

He noticed that the attractive glazier's daughter

passed him several times quite unconcerned, now and then adjusting the pink silk knot under her chin and fingering the beautiful lace of her neckerchief, which fell down over her breast. She talked freely with the other girls, and seemed very much at ease.

The cigar, like so many other things in this world, came to an end. The sergeant threw away the little stump, which was still afire, with the intention of tossing it into the lake; but the stump was so light that it went only a short distance on deck and lay there smoking. At once came a foot in the prettiest little polished shoe, and stepped on it, so that it was extinguished instantly. The sergeant raised his eyes from the foot to the head and saw the girl stranger. Her glances met his. He rose hurriedly from his trunk, approached her with a polite bow, and said: "Thank you, my dear girl! My cigar hardly deserved to be touched by your foot—but—"

A cold, scornful expression in her face was her answer. She turned her back upon him and went away.

"Then the devil take her!" With this thought, the sergeant, blushing and disheartened, leaped down the stairs into the dining-room. Here he crawled into the darkest corner, suitable for sleep or reflection. "Confound it, Albert!" he thought, and brushed the hair from his forehead. " I called

her 'my dear girl' and she didn't like that any better than when I called her 'Miss Videbeck' a little
while ago. What devilry!"

He was not alone in the room. He talked neither
loud nor low. But in order to display his courage
at once, both to himself and to the others, he called
out sternly and harshly to the waitress at the wicket:
"A cold meat sandwich, and be quick about it!"

The waitress came forth with the order on a tray.
"Go to the deuce with your sandwiches! Didn't I
ask for one with French bread?"

Obediently and politely she went back with the
tray and put the hard rye-bread sandwich on the
buffet.

"A glass of haut-brion, my girl! And don't let
me wait so long!"

The glass was filled and set on the tray together
with another sandwich made from an uncut French
roll.

"Do you think I am made to open my mouth
over a whole roll? In Stockholm we have sense
enough to cut a French roll in two and spread butter on each half."

The waitress went back again, took a knife, and
began to cut the sandwich.

"I beg — the deuce! — be so kind as to take a
new French roll, cut it in two, and spread butter
on the inside of each piece, please! Why, you've
got the butter right on the outside! Take another

roll! How one has to wait! Hang it — throw it all away, I am not hungry."

The girl at the buffet mumbled something sharp about "aristocratic travelers." This was not wholly displeasing to the sergeant; he came forward and paid for the sandwiches. "I ordered them," he said, "here is the money!"

"Your stomach is out of order — yes, certainly!" exclaimed a passenger dressed in black. The sergeant turned round, saw the collar and recognized the pale but shining face and the round light-blue bird-eyes of the pastor from Ulricehamn.

"Aha, how do you do! Why, this is Pastor Su — I presume you are going down to the country, are you not?"

"Yes, indeed."

"I am also going to Västergötland, though that does not mean home for me, but away from home," said the sergeant and mechanically seized his large, denounced, but purchased sandwich of the uncut roll, opening his mouth wide over it, and biting it vigorously.

"That's it," said the pastor; "one goes up country and the other down. I am going to Ulricehamn."

"Yes, and —" The sergeant emptied his glass of haut-brion, which stood waiting on the tray.

"As long as one enjoys good health, it is beneficial to travel back and forth like this," remarked the pastor.

"Oh, yes, yes." The sergeant now swallowed the last portion of his order.

"Are you leaving Stockholm for any great length of time, sergeant?"

"I have three months' leave of absence. May I offer you a glass of refreshment, pastor? What will you have? Porter or port wine?"

"Yes, indeed, one's stomach is unsettled on Lake Maelar. Well, if it must be, then either port wine or porter!"

The sergeant ordered both, and the pastor, unable to make a choice, drank both, ending with the warmest and most hospitable invitation to the young soldier to call at Ulricehamn and Timmelhed and be repaid.

The sergeant bowed, settled for the order, and darted back on deck in better spirits.

When he examined the shores they were passing, he noticed that the steamer was about to put into Strängnäs. Sailors far out on the lake can see the large cathedral and its majestic spire, which commands the whole Södermanland neighborhood. Only at close range can one discern a number of small red wooden houses straggling below the church; and the red-checkered college- and school-building alone rises high above the other shed-like hovels. When you finally land at the old, dilapidated wharf, you say to yourself, "This is Strängnäs."

Chapter II

" Here are no marks of aristocracy, none of the superiority of the higher peerage, none of the nobility of wealth in the rich and proud middle class, no signs of that primitive distinction found among the independent peasantry."

PASSENGERS landing at the pier see no well-developed harbor, no square, no real street, but only a hill; and most of the houses impolitely turn their gables toward the visitors. Nevertheless, since the steamer waits there about half an hour, they go ashore. Of course, they find none of the twisted buns for which Södertälje is famous; but if they climb carefully after their feet are planted on the wharf, keep their eyes open, and do not step in the holes between the rotten planks, they may get up town alive.

Among those who crossed the dock successfully were the sergeant and one other. As he stood on the fore-deck and watched the gangplank put out, he noticed a short way off the pink head with sparkling eyes looking up toward the little town. He quickly took courage, deciding to avoid all the pitfalls of addressing her by name or title.

" Look here!" he said, turning to her quite without restraint. " Look here! Let us go ashore! Come on! There is so much turmoil on the boat just now; they are going to take on wood and attend to other annoying things. Down in the dining-room it's

nasty, too; it's unpleasant to eat there because—
well— I know a very good place up here in Strängnäs. I think breakfast would taste pretty nice after
such a long fast."

She let him take her arm without ceremony,
passed over the gangplank and walked closer to
him on the unsafe pier, and presently they were in
Strängnäs.

"How I like this little town!" she said frankly,
and looked about cheerfully. "It is so different
from Stockholm."

"When you get on a little farther it is really
quite pleasant," replied the sergeant.

"Look—look," she continued. "Oh, I breathe
—but— I think—yes—yes, indeed. Lidköping
is still prettier."

The young soldier, who was delighted to note so
soon, and almost contrary to expectations, that his
acquaintance was a communicative person, began
to find Strängnäs very pleasant, as in fact it is.
Everything is unpretentious. Coming up from the
lake, one passes through only crooked, narrow lanes
or streets winding up the hills. No arrogant straight-
ness is to be seen in this community. The little
houses are old and friendly, and one soon observes
that they have not only gables, but also walls with
pretty windows in them, and even doors that one
feels inclined to enter. Here are no marks of aristocracy, none of the superiority of the higher peer-

age, none of the nobility of wealth in the rich and proud middle class, no signs of that primitive distinction found among the independent peasantry and exhibited in their manner of life. No, here are to be seen only civic conditions of the most unpretentious kind. One gets the impression that all the houses belong to skippers, glaziers, brush-makers, and fishermen.

Naturally, we refer here only to the part of Strängnäs that meets the passenger coming up from the lake and surrounds him until he reaches the tree-covered height about the cathedral. In that neighborhood, the bishop's house and a few other residences indicate a better district. But the sergeant and the glazier's daughter on his arm had not yet reached the height. They had not even come to the market-place. Because of her ejaculation on seeing the little house with the white shutters, they had stopped in that remarkable labyrinth of small, crooked streets and buildings which lies in Strängnäs between the shore and the market-place. Here the sergeant conducted his companion to a long flight of steps which led down from the street itself into a courtyard. They crossed the court to the door of a building. "Here," whispered the sergeant, "lives a rich dyer who keeps a pleasant, respectable restaurant. You will see how nice it is." The girl breathed as if in her own home, although she often remarked that Lidköping was still prettier.

They crossed the porch and entered. Inside the house, they went up a staircase to a large lunch room on the second floor. Sara Videbeck saw that it was a kind of tavern. The sergeant approached a neat, cheerful-looking person who was drying dishes behind the counter. "Let us have one of the small side rooms here—that on the right—or the one on the left—no matter—and breakfast. What have you got?"

"Raspberries and cream."

"Anything more substantial?"

"Roast woodcock—fresh salmon—"

"That'll do, but be quick! And," whispered the sergeant, while he conducted his acquaintance into the side room on the left, but in the door continued talking to the man with the dishes, "two glasses of cherry wine!"

When both had entered the little room and for the sake of greater comfort—in case others should enter the dining-room—had shut the door, Sara Videbeck took off her silk kerchief and exposed a head covered with dark brown glossy hair, well parted, and without any false curls near the temples (the sergeant remembered they had disappeared at the same time as the cambric hat), but with a couple of very neat ones of her own back of each ear. She took off her lilac-colored gloves also, and revealed two small, white, plump hands, which looked as though they had never done any coarse work, but which might bear the criticism of being a little too broad. They were provided with fingers which, though extremely pleasing and beautiful with tiny furrows in the joints, were nevertheless a bit fleshy. That these fingers had never played the lute, touched piano keys, wielded paintbrushes, or turned over the leaves of fine books, for which narrow and lithe finger-tips are required, the sergeant took for granted. It was still more plain that they had never used a spade, cleaned a stable, pounded washing, or done things of that sort. At the same time, he left it undecided whether or no they had kneaded putty in their day, because putty makes the skin white and soft. So much for the hands. In other respects her person was not short at all nor fat, but rather tall and quite slender.

The girl was not embarrassed, sitting alone with her sergeant. She broke off a small spray of lavender from a flower-pot in the window, rubbed it between her hands, and smelled of her fingers with gratification. The sergeant, not to be idle, broke off a geranium leaf and went through the same process for his own part.

"A pretty and very neat little room!" she exclaimed. "Yes, and what a fine chest of drawers! Is it walnut, I wonder, or oak? No, I believe it's polished pear-tree wood— can it be apple?"

The sergeant, who had never been familiar with carpenter shops, could give no information on this matter. Instead he turned to another subject and burst out: " 'Pon my word, a broad gilded frame around the mirror! That's old-fashioned now; it should be mahogany."

" Mahogany? Oh, not necessarily! I know a better way: to make the frame around the mirror of glass also, of thin, clear crown-glass, of pieces left over after cutting out the panes. You put them together to make a whole frame and place colored paper underneath. It makes a very pretty frame. You see, you look in the mirror itself to get the reflection, but look at the frame also for enjoyment, and you can put any kind of paper you wish underneath; they can be made very pretty. Have — have — you not seen them?"

Here she seemed a little puzzled about what she should call him. But just at this moment the order was brought in. A clean white, though not fine, table-cloth was spread on the table, and upon it were placed newly wiped plates.

"Just think if the steamer should go off and leave us!"

" Oh, no," answered the sergeant, "they fire a signal, and after the shot is fired we have plenty of time to get down to the dock."

The woman who had carried in the dishes of food had now gone out again, and the door was shut. The sergeant took his glass of cherry wine in his hand and said: "Here's to our trip!"

Without any ceremony, Sara Videbeck took the other little glass, touched that of her host, nodded jovially, and said, "Thank you!"

"Just a word before we drink," interposed the sergeant. "It is embarrassing and annoying not to know what to call each other — and then — I never want to make any one unhappy, angry, or vexed — so — I say, would n't you let me call you Sara — at least as long as we are breakfasting, or—"

"Sara? Yes, all right." With these words she touched his glass once more; the matter was settled, and the cherry wine was drunk. "By the way, how do you know that my name is Sara? I should also like to know what your first name is."

"Albert," answered the sergeant.

He felt like a newborn man after this burden had fallen from his breast; he walked around the room and became twice as free, happy, and courteous. But on the other hand, the pretty glazier's daughter did not undergo the slightest change. She sat at the table, ate and helped herself, in a very pleasant manner, it is true, but without showing any of the higher forms of grace in her movements. She called her new associate "Albert" at every eighth word without the slightest embarrassment due either to bashfulness or haughtiness. She seemed very much at home.

The sergeant, who felt himself superior at least with respect to manners, became all the happier from this feeling and said: " My dear Sara, have a few more raspberries! This cream is pretty good, is n't it?"

" Excellent! Thank you! I remember last summer down at the watering-place in Lund —"

He went out and ordered more raspberries.

At this moment the signal was fired on the steamboat.

" There," she said, got up, and put on her gloves. " Cancel the order of raspberries."

" My dear Sara, be seated! The raspberries will be here immediately, and we shall have plenty of time to get down to the dock."

" No, no! It is best to be prompt. Find out how much it costs!" she added, put on her head-dress, and pulled out a handkerchief from which the end of her purse protruded.

" What?" cried the sergeant. "It is I who —"

" Quick, quick!" She passed by him, went up to the desk in the dining-room herself, and asked the girl at the desk what the bill was.

" One rix-dollar and twelve pence."

" Here, my dear," — she pulled out her green silk purse, — " is one half of it. That 's my share!" Thereupon she nodded a good-by to the waitress who had carried in the food.

The nod both to the cashier and the waitress was polite, but of the supercilious kind, and seemed to indicate that she cared very little for either.

The sergeant for his part turned pale and was about to stammer forth that it was he who had done the inviting, and he would promptly pay. But Sara Videbeck was already in the doorway. Time was pressing. He paid his half, bit his lips with indignation, and passed out after her.

When they had come out on the doorstep, crossed over the courtyard, and were about to ascend the stairs to the street, she made a little motion from which it might be inferred that the sergeant ought to take her arm, which he did.

"Thank you for taking me to that nice place!" she said in an undertone with a most pleasing voice, and touched his hand as if for a gentle caress. "Does a rich dyer live here, did you say? Goodness!"

"Not at all," he answered. "Why, you paid for it yourself," he added to himself with mortification.

"Yes, I want to thank you very much; I was rather hungry. There are nice, kind people here wherever you turn; and the name of the city is Strängnäs?"

"Yes. I should like to take you around by the cathedral to see the more prominent parts of the town. Up there are beautiful shade-trees to walk under."

"Oh, dear me, no! We must get down to the steamboat. They are already waiting."

Now while they walked through the intersecting lanes with rapid steps, Sara nodded cheerfully to all the little corners she passed, and all of a sudden remarked: "Albert—let me see—I've read that name in the Almanac, have I not? Yes, and it was also the name given last summer to the master carpenter Ahlgren's son, to whom I was godmother. You will see he is a dear boy, Albe, his eyes bright as enamel."

"Your home is in Lidköping, I understand; I take it that you are on your way home?" the sergeant permitted himself to ask.

"Careful! Watch your step!" she said, for they were right on the dangerous wharf just now. But they crossed the gangplank without any mishap, and found themselves again on the steamer. It put off, and the paddle-wheels began to revolve. Clouds of smoke and a dull noise formed the swimming dragon's farewell to Strängnäs.

Chapter III

THE sergeant had made up his mind to pay his new acquaintance some attention. Therefore he went down to the dining-room and asked for a pound of candy. "It is never sold on steamboats," was the answer.

"That so? The deuce! Have you any oranges here? Seems to me I can see some lying over there in the basket."

"Yes."

"Good! Give me four."

When he came up with the fruit in his hand, he found the deck occupied and arranged as follows: the large portion of the better class—men, wives, and children—had gone down into the dining-room. To be sure, there were a few couples at the stern, but they were not exactly engaged in lively conversation, and though not entirely asleep, were absolutely indifferent to everything around them. The women from Dalecarlia nearest the bow seemed to be reclining on the circular heaps of hawsers, slumbering. The four or five maid-servants already mentioned had gathered with their backs against the half-unfolded sail. The captain was presumably in his cabin; he was not seen on deck. The machinists worked on in their prison.

"But where is my pink friend?" the sergeant asked himself.

He finally discovered her sitting on a green bench near the railing in the recess behind one of the superstructures over the paddle-wheels. The sergeant found such an isolated place quite agreeable, went there with his oranges, sat down beside her, and invited her to have one.

She nodded a kind of assent and pulled out her purse.

"Well, I'll be damned!" thought the sergeant, with the blood rushing to his face, "do you suppose she is going to pay me for those oranges at once, and in cash? This here lower class can go—"

But it did not turn out so bad as that. She pulled out a knife with a handle of Britannia metal from her crocheted purse and peeled an orange with it, which she politely handed to Albert. Then she peeled one for herself, cut it in six parts, and began to eat it with a relish.

"Thank you, my dear Sara!" said Albert, as he received his orange.

Thereupon he asked, and was permitted, to borrow her knife to cut up his own fruit. He inspected the knife with a certain feeling of wonder; it was, in truth, very dull. The point was almost round, without resembling that of a table-knife. In other respects it was new and quite sharp on one edge. He did not pay much more attention to it, but said after a moment: "Now, Sara, we must get better acquainted, and you must tell me how closely you are related to your aunt, the one who —"

"Failed to come along this morning? It will not be difficult, I think, to tell how closely I am related to my mother's sister."

"Of course not, but—"

"I am very sorry that she did n't come, poor Aunt Ulla; now she has been obliged to hire a team of her own or travel with the Gothenburg stage, and it remains to be seen where we can meet on the way, if at all. Perhaps she 'll stay in Stockholm now, since she had such a mishap in the very beginning. You must know that I have another unmarried aunt by the name of Gustava; she lives in Lidköping and looks after my sick mother while I am away. But this Aunt Ulla has long been a resident of Stockholm, and she was only to take a trip home with me in order to wake herself up a bit, and it was stupid that she should be late, though that happens quite often to poor Aunt Ulla. I was also sorry for my own sake; it is always good to have an aunt or somebody like that along when one is traveling. Yet I was sure, for all that, that I should n't fail to find some passenger on the way who—Eat yourself, Albe! I can't eat up all these alone."

"Thank you," he said, glad that he, too, might say a word. "Do you come to Stockholm often?

It is certainly a long distance to Stockholm from Lidköping!"

"I have never been to Stockholm before. It was necessary for me this time to be on the lookout for oil and diamonds and to examine the latest style."

The sergeant looked at the girl in wonder and was silent. "Oil," he thought; "I must have been entirely mistaken about her condition. Hm! The latest style?" He measured her figure from top to toe. It was really quite elegant, too, that is, of its kind. Finally he said in a low voice, "Diamonds?"

"Yes, just diamonds, sir! Ha-ha—perhaps you think that flint will do, eh? No, sir. Flint will do to strike fire, as in the lock of a musket. But, you see, whoever wants to cut glass, sir, must have a diamond!"

Her eyes opened wide and sparkled at these words, as if from a high, inborn self-assurance. She seemed almost proud, although pride never appeared in her glance except when she turned her back on some one. Besides, she sank down immediately to the plane of intimacy again when she noticed that Albert in his amazement was about to drop his orange. She went on: "Formerly we always used to get our chalk from Gothenburg and could have done so with the oil also; but my mother received a letter stating that it could be had in Stockholm for sixpence less per half-gallon, and then I found pleasure in coming up here and investigating,

since I had an aunt here already with whom I could
stay. But I care nothing about this new style of color-
ing glass for church windows, which they are said to
have invented in Stockholm, and which they talked
so much about in Lidköping. I did n't see any of it
in Stockholm. I purposely visited all the churches
in that city, and it was not an easy task, because
there are such an awful lot of them; but there
was n't colored glass in a single one. I don't know
where that falsehood originated, unless it should be
in Uppsala, where a professor is said to be painting
the windows in a chancel. Naturally, I wanted to
learn it; because we have many orders for church
windows, both for — yes — and way down near
Skara. You see, in Skara there is nobody who can
treat glass, and ·I knew that it would be a fine big
income if we could color glass in our shop. We
should then be the only glaziers near enough who
could do anything with the new fad, and they would
buy from us as soon as anything was broken in the
churches. But I will pay no attention to it now; I
hear that the custom is not practiced anywhere, and
then it is not worth anything. I got some fine diamonds, though, so that I am quite satisfied with
my trip, and then oil — "

"But what in the name of heaven do you use
so much oil for?"

"For putty, of course. What else in the world
do you think oil is used for?"

"But why does n't your father himself take these long and important business trips?"

"Oh, heavens, he died six years ago."

"That's a different matter."

"And since then my mother, poor thing, has had charge of the shop — with the rights of a widow, of course; so I can say that I alone look after things."

"But tell me, my pretty Sara, how old are you, if I may ask?"

"A little over twenty-four."

"What, is it possible? I took you to be eighteen. With those cheeks — that complexion —"

"Yes, I had those same cheeks at eighteen. They say that young ladies in the upper class pretend to be younger than they are, at least I heard that was the custom at the watering-place in Lund; but I see little honor in looking old when you are young. I think it is much better the other way round. And about how old — if I may ask?"

"Am I? We are about the same age. I am twenty-five years old."

"And I took you for a person of only about nineteen, who had not yet risen from the ranks. You act so straightforward."

"The ranks? Well, my dear, to be honest, I have not risen from them yet, and probably never shall."

"What — what are you, then?"

"Just a non-commissioned officer."

"I have seen some before among people from Skaraborg, and they were respectable men. I remember near Lund Springs—there were some women loafers there, young ladies who pretended to drink mineral water for this, that, and the other; at that time there was also a swarm of lieutenants, captains, majors, and people of that kind, whom they called officers, from Västergötland and Skaraborg. These also pretended to be feeling ill and talked to the young ladies. But if I ever saw any non-commissioned officers at the Lund watering-place, they were always first-rate fellows with a real sickness, who did not drink for pleasure."

"But what were you doing then at Lund Springs, Sara? I suppose you, being well, had just gone there to enjoy the beautiful scenery?"

"I was there only one day and earned some money by selling boxes. I had to go there to look after a couple of our apprentices, who had been sent for to put in a lot of window-panes in the assembly room that had been knocked out during a peculiar game of ball between the guests on the fourth of July. You can never depend on the boys; they break the material, don't understand how to cut it, and manipulate the diamond poorly. Since this was a job of considerable importance, I went there myself, and I don't regret it. What do you suppose, Albe? I put in fifty-six small panes: twenty-two of inferior green glass, and listen!—thirty-four of

beautiful broad glass. Besides that, I sold ten glass
boxes, such as are made only by us in our shop,
with stripes of gilt paper underneath, and six big
lanterns, which they use when they go down into
the cellars for Seltzer water, broth, cheap refreshments, and things of that sort. As I was saying, I
saw only two non-commissioned officers there, serious fellows with gout, both of them from Västergötland Valley. How does it come about that you
can be a non-commissioned officer and still be so
young?"

"In Stockholm the younger non-commissioned
officers are sometimes accustomed to — especially
since—well, you see, I am not very different from
an officer—I am a sergeant."

"Sergeant? Well, that's good enough as it is.
Never mind becoming a commissioned officer, a
lieutenant, or anything else like that. Those idlers
never do anything but talk rubbish to the young
ladies in the daytime and to the servant girls at
night-time. Trash! 'Frills galore; nothing more.'"

The soldier sat half-frightened at hearing the elo-
quence and bold sallies of his open-hearted friend.
He knew, with respect to himself, that he was only
too willing to become a lieutenant, and hoped
to win this promotion through his secret kinship
with a certain prominent family in the capital.
He knew also that he had sufficient funds for
the present to make that inspection trip to certain

estates on which he had been sent out during his summer furlough. Therefore he did not feel inclined to apply to himself those gloomy rhymes about frills and so on. But he could not deny that the laughing and talking with ladies and servant girls had given him pleasure now and then. He looked perplexed at Sara with her decisive utterances. He examined her face; her happy and friendly eyes seemed to contradict her last severe words. In fact, when he looked upon the red, full, almost beautifully formed lips, with the regular, whitely gleaming teeth between, and the little tip of a deep-red tongue that peeped out occasionally, a man like him might well be pardoned for the silent question: "Has nobody in this world ever kissed that mouth?"

Sara looked into his face also, as he into hers, and finally she asked in a clear, mild voice : "What are you looking at so intently?"

Quite unexpectedly and boldly he answered: "I am just wondering whether any person has ever kissed that mouth."

A quickly flitting smile was her only answer, and she looked away over the Maelar waters. In so doing, there was not the slightest coquettishness or glimmer of mischief discernible in her eye, but, on the other hand, nothing exactly romantic or dreamily divine. It was an intermediate something of an incomprehensible character. Not at all ugly, nor yet profoundly beautiful. It was of the kind concerning which we are wont to express ourselves with a happy countenance: "Oh, it will do!"

Encouraged that she did not spurn him or, at least, turn her back on him and go away, the sergeant continued: "I could give you much talk, my dear Sara, of the same calibre as what you have told me is used in speaking to young ladies. Indeed, I feel that I am not a stranger to that kind of prattle. But you have made it clear to me how much you hate it. I will not even mention *heart*, since I remember my experience earlier to-day — and besides, I believe, to speak frankly, that your heart is of glass; and as for me, I do not possess the diamond, the only weapon that will make an impression on it."

"Are you going to stop in Arboga, Albert, where the steamer arrives to-night?" This she asked with a piercing glance.

"I? Not at all. I am going down to the district of Vadsbo, to certain estates, and then perhaps still farther into Västergötland."

"Then we'll go together" — again a piercing glance — "then we can have two horses and a two-horse carriage — and club together — and — because I see you have no vehicle of your own with you. Farmers' gigs are hard to ride in, and postboy-codgers sitting beside me are not to my taste; they are seldom clean."

The sergeant sprang up and would probably have pressed her in his arms if they had not been on deck. "She has a heart," he thought.

"Sit down, Albert, and we will amuse ourselves by figuring out the cost of our conveyance. Help me, if I make a mistake. My greatest delight is to add in my head. Let's see, now: the first distance, counting from Arboga, is to Fellingsbro?"

The sergeant sat down beside her, gay and spirited as if he had just received a commission. And at this moment, he thought, she was just as beaming or, more correctly, just as charmingly beautiful as a girl — according to his taste — ever could be. She was so sensible and wise and yet so captivating.

"Well, are you not going to answer me?" she said and gently struck his hand with one of her lilac-colored gloves, which she had cautiously removed earlier when she was peeling the orange.

"Quite right, the road goes to Fellingsbro and from there to Glanshammar," he said.

"And then to Vretstorp?"

"No, no. We must go through Örebro and Kumla first."

"And then Vretstorp, that is certain. Then Bodarna and Hofva, and then we are home."

"What, is your home in Hofva?"

"My home is in Västergötland, and as soon as I put my foot in Hofva, I shall be home directly."

Here Sara stretched out one of her little feet and set it down on deck in a very definite Västergötland way.

Albert had a new opportunity to admire the well-made, pretty shoe. "Is that Lidköping work?" he asked.

"What's that?"

"I mean, do they have such good shoemakers in Lidköping that —"

"That's indeed a fine, delightful town! Have you never been in Lidköping? Shoemakers—I should say so! We have tailors, blacksmiths, white-smiths, cabinet-makers, carpenters; we have every-thing. We have merchants also and a rich inn-keeper on the street to the left of the market-place; although I disapprove of that, because such people live on the ruin and the unnecessary expenditures of others. But the skilled artisan does something worth while and permanent in this world. What becomes of the innkeeper's commodities? He is a commissioner for the Gothenburg stage and keeps a great big ballroom, where officers hold assemblies with ladies. You ought to see those balls! But I don't approve of that hotel business anyway. If people were only respectable, such folks would soon have to move out of Lidköping. But now many want to drink, play, and dance, and — there is a tremendously large ballroom there, Albert! If I remember correctly, there are eight bay-windows lengthwise and twenty-four panes in every bay."

"Don't you like to dance at all, Sara?"

"When I have looked after the shop, finished my work, and can be alone, it happens sometimes that I dance; but it is without a violin."

"She is a genuine Västergötland product!" thought the sergeant, though at this moment she looked so infinitely sweet, so appealing, that he remained silent. Shortly afterward he added: "To think that your mother is so sick! Suppose she should be dead, Sara, when we get — when you get down there?"

"Would to God that might be so, poor thing! She has never had any real happiness in this life. Anxiety and sorrow and now, finally, nothing but sickness. It is a pretty bad condition, Albert."

"You talk too distressingly. If she should die, what would happen to your shop?"

"Well, that would be the end of the legal privileges, and I cannot get any from the magistrate, I know that. But I have thought out a plan just the same."

"Indeed?"

"Yes, I don't mind telling you about that," she continued, moved yet a little closer to Albert on the bench, and looked about, as if fearing that some stranger might overhear her secrets. But since this part of the deck, as stated before, was free from people, she turned to him again, looked very wise and confidential, and waved her little glove in the air, at times gently striking his arm with it.

"I have found out how a girl like myself, without parents or brothers and sisters, can live — and live well," she said. "I am already amply provided with linen and wearing apparel for many years to come, and I don't wear them out fast; one does n't when one is careful. Now when my mother dies I shall not be allowed to cut out window-panes any more or to putty in large houses and new buildings; that's for the master of the guild. But there is a unique art, I tell you, which nobody knows in Lidköping except myself, because I alone have discovered it: that of mixing chalk with oil in proper dimen — no, proportions — dimensions are applied to the length and breadth of the glass itself, but proportion is applied to the correct mixture and quality of chalk and oil together; those two words are used only in our trade, and you don't understand them, Albert — Well, I only want to tell you that I have discovered a proportion of this preparation which no one knows but myself, and which forms a putty so strong that the severest autumn rainstorm cannot dissolve it. I shall prepare that and sell it to all the official masters of the trade; because they will want to buy it both in Lidköping and Vänersborg and Mariestad, too, once they know about it. And they know about it already, because I have had my assistants noise it abroad on their trips. At home I shall have it for sale in my room.".

"But as an unmarried woman you are unprotected, and—"

"We shall see. On the contrary, if I had a husband as unsober and irritable as my mother's was, I should be defenceless and miserable. No, I tell you, I shall get along just as I am. We ourselves own a little place on the Lida River. It is a rather small wooden house, like one of those up there in Strängby —Sträng—how was it—why—"

"Strängnäs.".

"And when mamma dies, the place will pass to me. Poor mother! She will live a couple of years yet, and when she does die, I know from what the mayor told me that with a house and lot I need no other protection, though single. The house does not rent for very much; yet I can let a couple of rooms upstairs and live on the ground floor myself. But since I am accustomed to having a good time and being among people, I don't want to sit by myself all the time, so I intend to open a shop —a little store—with trade such as women may take care of, which has n't yet been put under the guild. In my store I intend to sell boxes, fine pretty glass boxes with colored paper pasted underneath— I have made them for several years, and the country people all around here are passionately fond of them —and besides that, lanterns. In fact, I have learned

how to cover glass with foil, and from that I intend
to make little mirrors for people in the parishes.
Perhaps I'll take in all kinds of odds and ends, too,
into my shop to sell on commission, such as cloth,
linen, handkerchiefs, neckwear, and home-made
goods, so long as I don't touch silk, which is con-
trolled by the guild. It will not be such a small
business, when people are well treated at the counter; and I'll sit in my store from ten in the morning
till five in the afternoon; to stay longer would not
be worth while. Before ten in the morning, before
I open the store, I shall mix the putty for all the
master glaziers. It will be a good business and a
happy life!"

Sara's eyes, mouth, and cheeks lighted up when
she said this. But the sergeant asked: "Do you intend, then, to stay indoors all the year round and
never look outside or breathe the delightful country air?"

"At sunrise I take a walk out toward Trufve. I
do that every morning in the summer time when
the weather is clear."

"Tru—what may that be?"

"Why, Trufve; that is Richert's beautiful estate
on the way to Mariestad. If only the road from the
city out in that direction were not so horribly
sandy! Yet I don't care very much; I don't use
it very often. Many mornings I prefer to stay at
home. I have salvia and roses in the windows, and

I am going to get some pots of lavender. Besides, I can see the Lida through the windows, and there is no river more beautiful. If I want to see more water, I have the great Lake Vänern tó gaze upon when I look through my windows in the direction of the gap near Kålland Island; the latter I can see by just turning my eyes toward the Municipal Bridge."

"And when you become old, my dear Sara?"

"If I live until I am fifty, I expect to travel around to fairs with my goods. As long as I am young, it is better to stay at home in my little store."

"People like to trade at a counter where there is such a sweet saleslady," he remarked.

"But at my age it is disagreeable to attend fairs," she continued, turning her face away a trifle. "One encounters—When I am fifty, then I think it will be past; then, on the other hand, business is liable to be poorer in my store, and I shall try the fairs, if I have not before that time laid by a sum, as I hope to have, so that I can live without worry. For one can live simply and still feel very well, as long as—" Her face dropped, and her countenance darkened.

"Well, for heaven's sake! What do you mean?"

"Well, I mean, provided one takes care not to have a tormentor who eats up and squanders needlessly and carelessly all that one accumulates with so much pains and trouble. What good does it do to be orderly when the tormentor is all the more disorderly and feasts upon the labors of the industrious woman? And how can one work with a will without joy of heart and when full of stifling anxiety —"

"I don't understand you."

"You don't? Hm."

"For God's sake, tell me what you mean!"

"Well, that is something to tell, I think. I was out one Michaelmas night with my mother; it was windy, and her hair was blowing about her hood. In despair she ran up toward the Municipal Bridge, which passes over the Lida at home in our town; I was fifteen years old then and ran after. I thought she would jump down into the water in her terrible anguish. But when I came after, she checked herself and took me in her arms, stopped at the hand-rail, and looked round. 'For your sake I'll desist,' she whispered. 'I will live and be tormented until you become a little bigger. But woe and curses upon this thing here! I will get rid of *that* anyway.' At that, I believe, I saw a froth of rage about my mother's lips; she took the gold ring from her finger and hurled it far out into the Lida River."

The sergeant turned pale; he was reminded of something that had taken place that morning near the railing of the steamer.

"Your mother seems to have been a little impatient in the married state," remarked the sergeant.

"Shame—shame on you—sir!" exclaimed Sara with flashing glances. "Albert!" she added soon after, in a milder voice. "A horse that has been kicked twenty times and turns and kicks back the twenty-first time is not impatient. And it is true before God," she said finally, with a hardly audible but fervent and sonorous voice, "that there was one who was continually exhorting and preaching and saying that my mother would be all the better—or *nobler*, I believe they call it—by this torture, but that was a lie. Because she became worse year after year, I know that much. From being the cleanest and most orderly person she became at last untidy, disagreeable, and careless, so that I used to weep over it." Here Sara wept. "Though once a pious and God-fearing person, she finally would n't look in the prayer-book—and—lately—oh—"

"Calm yourself!"

"Up to this very day my mother has been in bed, and do you know what from? God help us—drunkenness. That's not right for a woman, Albert."

The sergeant rose, felt a cold perspiration under his doublet, took it off, and fanned himself with his handkerchief. Perhaps a few of his best plans crossed each other at this moment within his mind. But he was young and had no hardened heart. He had pity on these human beings; nor was he suffi-

ciently half-learned to come forward with the customary false phrases about bad being good. Seized
by a feeling of wonder and astonishment, he nevertheless approached a subject which military men
seldom touch on; he sat down confidentially beside his friend, who had so suddenly become open-
hearted, and asked: "Tell me truly and frankly,
Sara, are you what they generally call a Dissenter?"

"A Dissenter—oh, no, certainly not. There are
enough of them in Västergötland without me."

"But you sometimes read the Bible?"

"The Bible? Yes."

"Then you know God's first great general commandment—forgive me, it sounds a little—'be
fruitful, and multiply, and replenish the earth!'
Shall not this commandment be obeyed?"

After a little consideration, but without embarrassment, she answered: "Why, that commandment of God means—"

"That man and wife shall be together—"

"But it does n't mean that a man shall live together with just any woman in the world—that I
am sure of, nor that a woman shall be united to
any man that comes her way through a variety of
circumstances and accidents. If I remember correctly, it is intended as a help to man; therefore
it does not purpose to bring about his destruction,
does it? The destruction of both body and soul, and
most of all the soul! No, just as we must avoid and

escape great danger, misfortune, and distress, and
above all eschew bad and ruinous company, we
ought most certainly to be allowed to flee from—"

All of a sudden, a loud creaking was heard from
the forepart of the steamer, and the captain and a
machinist came running. But it was nothing more
than a hawser that had broken, whereby the little
distended sail began to flutter a bit carelessly, sway-
ing back and forth for a moment in the wind.
They had now come to one of the large basins of
Lake Maelar, Spruce Bay, where, upon crossing to
Blacken, there is almost always a strong breeze. On
account of the more violent rocking, all the passengers were set moving: the deck was filled with a
number of faces that had not been seen all day, but
which now, like cave-dwellers, came up from their
lower world, the saloon. After fluttering a few minutes, the sail was gathered in and set anew according to the direction of the wind. All became quiet
again, although the wind was not gentle. But ves-
sels that move by virtue of an inner fire care very
little for wind or wave; they go their steady path forward whether the wind is for or against, or whether,
as now, it blows from one side. In Spruce Bay there
are many dangerous places, concealed rocks, and
lurking ridges; wherefore many ships were wrecked
here at the time when they sailed without fire and
often had to manœuvre about. Then the most skillful navigator, in spite of his knowledge of bays and

reefs, was unable to avoid them at all times, because, except for the steering-gear, he had nothing
at his disposal but big, wide, heavy, wind-tossed
sails. Whatever way he turned or manœuvred
them, they often rushed off with him in a direction
he did not want to go; for a poor helmsman on a
sloop is after all but a man. Now, when the vessel
is driven by steam, one goes straight ahead, whether
the sails will or no, using them only when the wind
is from such a direction that it can serve as motive power. The steersman, to be sure, must still
know the marks and lurking cliffs; but knowing
where they are he can easily avoid them, if he is not
a fool. The only great danger in steam navigation
is from fire; in the construction of the boiler precautions can be taken against this, however, so that
it seldom happens.

They traveled along at a good speed, but the
natural consequence of the excitement on deck was
that the sergeant and Sara were interrupted in their
discussion of humanity's greatest problem.

The sergeant, impelled by his active nature, had
run up and caught hold of the sail, to the great
pleasure and satisfaction of the skipper. The result
was an invitation to drink a pledge of friendship
below deck in the captain's cabin. Our story omits
entirely the details of the dinner on the vessel, for
a deck passenger knows little about it. He notices
only from the sun's descent toward the horizon

and the lively running of the waitresses with filled cups of coffee that dinner must be over. The drawing-room inhabitants have established that custom among themselves; and when a few cave-dwellers' figures, a little happier than usual, or at least not so dark under their eyes, came up from their hiding-place about this time, the fore-deck passengers could understand that the gentry had had refreshments. Yet it is true, as this narrative has pointed out before, that now and then a male deck passenger of a bolder nature may at least go down into the dining-room, quickly and merrily get a mouthful, and come up again. But the women who belong to the people really have a hard time. The historiographer has wondered many a time how they live over there on the fore-deck. It is not considered entirely proper that they take food along to feed themselves. Of the common abundant fare which is prepared in the steamer kitchen they generally get nothing, since they have nothing better than deck accommodations. It may happen that even among these women some one of sufficient daring is found to descend into the world of the cave-dwellers and obtain a tidbit, whereupon she ascends again into the fresh air. Yet it is not considered modest of her to do so. A charitable custom is serving coffee, which is not food, but very good nevertheless, at about four or five o'clock. It comes of itself from the cave beneath and is handed around on deck by waitresses, who may be spoken to, if not too sulky, so that even a poor deck mortal may get a cup. Sara was on hand and actually got one; then, too, she looked so well and neat that, except for the headgear, the coffee-bearers would willingly have counted her among the higher class ladies. It was certainly hard to understand that she, whose purse with silver coins had been noticed several times, had not bought a saloon ticket and become a cave-dweller like the others. This must have come about through her love of the open air and her dislike of bad air and caves in general.

While she was drinking her coffee and deciding to ask for a second cup, she remembered with fervent pleasure and gratitude Sergeant Albert's suggestion to take her on shore to that pleasant little town — she had forgotten the name again — with the small, red-painted cottages. There she had enjoyed getting, without any difficulties, a good, hearty meal. In spite of its name of breakfast, it had meant dinner for her and, now that the coffee had appeared, made her feel satisfied, happy, and free. The sergeant himself had a more ravenous appetite, and, just as he had sought aid from the buffet for the hardships which he endured during the forenoon, so now we find him there again. This new friendship with the captain permitted him to pass up and down at any time without fear and as often as he wished. One needed a special knowledge of his ticket to guess that he did not really belong to the gentry but to the people. What, how, when, and where he ate is not revealed; it is merely surmised that he had dinner. He was young, with healthy requirements such as God has created, but he was by no means a gourmand or drinker and was not voracious, disgusting, or in other respects a cave-dweller. Then, too, he did not seem to like the cabin caves: as soon as he could he came up and left them. He must have been a particular friend of the air that was blowing on the fore-deck, because that is where he stayed most of the time, and where he had lighted his cigar again.

Chapter IV

"Then he sank down in his chair with a heavy heart, and rested his head against the back. 'You are without a diamond, Albert! Close your eyes and go to sleep and modify your pretensions!'"

SARA VIDEBECK was looking after her things, which she kept in carpet-bags on the fore-deck. She seemed to be particularly solicitous about one of them; for once, when there was no other person so far forward, she took an opportunity to tap the smoker on the arm and say: "Albert, you won't mind if I ask a little favor of you, will you? I have a bag here, the one with the brass initials S. V.; see to it that no one sits down on it! From the very start and all day, I have kept it under the sail, but on the last inspection tour they pulled out various things; the sail is up, and my traveling-bag is exposed."

Albert took the cigar out of his mouth, looked at her, and said: "Is the carpet-bag so sensitive that not even so light a body as yours may rest on it? Otherwise it could be guarded best that way."

"No, no indeed, neither I nor you, and least of all anybody else."

"Is it full of diamonds?"

"Oh my, no!"

"Well, what then? Forgive me, it's none of my business. Don't worry, be happy, and go wherever you like! I'll guard your bag."

Sara thanked him with a look as if the carpet-bag had been her own heart. She went away to busy herself with certain boxes that she had placed to one side on the deck.

"I wonder what the girl has in that bag!" thought Albert, as he stood looking down on the shining, yellow S. V., and drew an enormously large cloud of smoke from his cigar. "She is, nevertheless, a rich girl, I am sure; there is no doubt about it. I don't care a bit about that though, I'll get enough money from"—here he mumbled a mysterious family name—"and from the estates in Vadsbo, where I have my definite percentage as manager. The initials are pretty well made; they have brass-smiths in Lidköping that are worth while. Shall I accompany her all the way there? Otherwise I ought to turn off from the main highway at Mariestad and go inland. Well, we'll see. It's a long way yet — See here, you girl with the tray! Bring me up a new cigar! I don't want to leave the place.—Oh, the deuce, she did n't hear me! How will this end? Then I'll smoke a little farther on this stump, but it tastes hot, and the smoke goes up in my nose, when—damn it! The traveling-bag is not particularly large; quite long but not broad; she surely has glass boxes in it, since no one may sit down on it. But who the deuce would be impudent enough to sit down on it? I have never seen the rest of the deck rabble sit down on any-

thing except the cordage, pump, and cannon.
They 're very gentle, kind folk. They take so little
liberty with other people's goods that the Dalecarlian women, for instance, sit down on themselves
only, that is, they put their legs under their bodies.
What impudent individual could Sara have feared
who would have dared — aha — you 'll see, Albert,
that she meant you yourself and none other when
she made that beautiful appeal to you to watch her
bag. Great Lucifer, what a taste!" he exclaimed and
threw the last remnant of the stump into the lake.
" This beats my patience."

Just in this difficult crisis Sara came up to him
and —what do you think? —put a fresh cigar into
his hand. " I have no light with me," she said. " I
didn't want to let the maid from whom I bought
the cigar light it for you, because—and besides she
does n't smoke. But how will you light it, Albe?"

"Oh, I 'll show you," he remarked; "here comes
the captain of the craft walking with his excellent
trabucos in his mouth. Pardon me, my dear captain,
—kindly step a little nearer so that I can light my
cigar. This pretty girl has assigned me to a post
which, as a good soldier, I am not able to leave."

" Just a moment, just a moment!" answered the
captain. Sara stood and looked on, and she could
not help laughing aloud when the two men put the
ends of their cigars against each other, watched
them with serious eyes, and puffed vehemently to

get a light. The attempt was successful, and the honorable, jovial captain went on his way. With an expression of particular happiness, the sergeant filled both cheeks chock-full of new, fresh smoke— for every one knows that it is the first whiff of smoke that tastes the best—and blew it out very slowly, but in his absent-mindedness right into Sara's face.

"O-oh," she cried, and ran away to the other part of the fore-deck to attend to the previously mentioned boxes.

Consequently Albert again stood alone by his traveling-bag, that is to say, hers, and contemplated the mild, beautiful setting of the sun. They had now come to Galten, at the end of the Maelar basin, in the direction of Arboga. Albert stood watching the sun, as we have said, but now and then he looked at the bag also. He smoked more slowly now, for he thought: "If this cigar should be finished all of a sudden, it is not likely that I shall get another as conveniently as this one. Yes, most assuredly she has glass in her bag, and I like that better than if she had glass in her breast or her whole heart were made of it, as I believed once. That was a stupid thought of mine—puh!—but I shall not blow out too much smoke at a time—puh!— What if her soul is of glass to some extent, can't I have a diamond and cut it as well as anybody else? But I shall not cut deep; the devil would n't have the heart to do that on such a beautiful crystal—puh!—I shall just engrave an *A* upon the enamel for her memory; I might be allowed to do that, I should think. It is n't too much—puh!—She is pretty when she is solemn, but prettier still when she smiles that way, and she was prettiest of all when she wept over her mother. It is strange I should like that. One generally looks ugly when one whines—puh!—But the corners of her eyes did n't get red, they were as clear as — Well, the weeping did n't last long anyway."

"Ease the ship, ease the ship!" yelled the captain to the helmsman. "Don't you see that buoy, you rascal? Well, it 's beginning to get dark," he added good-naturedly. "It is best now for me to relieve him from steering and go there myself. The mouth of the Arboga is not like other harbors. Alee! Ship alee! For God's sake, stop the engine! Get down from there, I 'll take your place myself. Tell them to take in the jib!"

"Stop her, stop!" was heard in answer. The vessel slowed up, and the skillful captain, who now stood at the helm himself, had time to right her course so that the danger point was passed successfully.

The innermost strait of Lake Maelar at its western end, in front of the Kungsbarkarö and Björkskog parishes, is full of small shoals, treacherous reefs, and promontories, which are always troublesome to the seafarer. These jutting bits of land nearest Arboga River are a continuation of the low Kungsör meadows that spread like a green carpet in the west and almost seem to steal down beneath the water, so that, especially at night, it is impossible to see any well-defined boundary line between the grassy shore and the lake. In that case, a sailor fixes his direction from the roof of Kungsör Castle, which is situated but a short distance from the mouth of the river. This time, as always, *Yngve Frey* proceeded without a mishap.

Just as the steamer entered the river, a deep, dry voice up in the stern was heard speaking to his neighbor: "How far is it now to the city?" "About nine miles," replied another voice with an expression of extreme politeness and eagerness. The voice was a soprano, like a woman's, but yet was a man's. "Good!" exclaimed the bass, and looked at his watch. "It is seven o'clock, we'll be there by eight, or at least by nine, and may expect good food and real beds." These words passed between two fathers of families. "If you require it, baron," said the soprano (also a baron), "it will be an easy matter, very easy, if we take the opportunity at Kungsör and send a courier to the city by land to engage rooms for us, for at this time there are a great many travelers."

"Can that be done, captain?" asked the bass-voiced aristocrat carelessly. "Oh, yes, certainly, certainly, of course," interrupted the soprano eagerly, before the captain at the helm had time to answer.

"It can be done," said the latter, "though not without a little inconvenience."

"In what way?" asked the bass, tired of so much talking.

"Yes, I tell you — without a difficulty, quite conveniently, very easily!" The soprano ejaculated with the most rapid utterance possible. The honorable captain at the helm looked about seriously. "Yes," he said, "a boat may still put ashore, and at the inn up there engage a man to ride to the city, if it is necessary. But I hope we shall be there as soon as he."

"Oh, yes, yes, oh, yes," said the soprano, "we shall arrive at the landing-place just as soon, I presume, with the help of our good captain. But afterward much time is lost, wasted, and consumed by landing, so that it is always a good thing — What do you say, baron? Shall we send a courier to reserve and occupy all the rooms?"

"All right!" said the sleepy bass, and he tucked his chin down into his coat. The soprano jumped up like a happy greyhound, but not farther than to the captain at the helm, which was very near. "Give the order, my dear captain, give the order, the order!"

The captain, good-natured though he was, seemed annoyed by this fuss, but would not, nevertheless, displease the barons, and called one of his men. "Get the skiff ready and go ashore and —" He gave the man the message. "You will have to follow us afterwards."

"Yes, the baron will pay for the trouble, of course, of course, of course!" muttered the soprano, turning toward the captain, and half pointing to the bass, who was slouching down into his coat.

"It is worth something," answered the captain firmly, stroking his chin and looking away at the shores between which he was steering. The view on the right was extensive and attractive. The meadows to an immeasurable distance north and northwest were covered with a million hay-cocks, like the small uncut knots on the reverse side of a large green piece of fancy needlework.

"And all this Hörstadius has acquired! He is certainly quite a pastor!" said the captain with a nod, as he stood talking to himself. "That man will become either immensely wealthy or immensely poor before he dies. He is a minister who preaches with hay. He can say, as the Scriptures do: 'What is hay is flesh,' because with such a good lease he has an extraordinary income. The Land Revenue or the War Department — I don't know which — has been very kind to him. But I wonder at the way he has acquired estates in all provinces: not only in Kungsör, but also in Södermanland, in fact all

over the kingdom. Has n't he leaseholds way off
deuce-and-gone in desolate Uppland, in Sollen-
tuna? I tell you Hörstadius is an economist! Then
he torments his poor body by riding round on a
farmer's gig and knocking about his whole life between his tenant farms to look after things. It must
be a damnably hard job to look after farms in every
province. While he jolts around in that way, he is
still so hard on his own body that he will drink only
water. Hörstadius is from Västergötland, that's the
trouble. They're certainly peculiar people in that
section! But what I commend in him is this: that
he is said to be so honest and kind toward all his
thousand overseers, hired men, and inspectors, that
in the end he seems to torment nobody more than
himself. Take in the sail, hoist the flag! No, the
navigator of a steamboat is less of a martyr. Come
over here! Come and steer! I am going down. The
river is clear now all the way to Arboga and easy to
navigate."

The mate came as ordered, and the captain
turned over the helm to him and went away. He
walked across the deck and downstairs to the lower
quarters, where the toddy was just ready and steam-
ing. There was punch there also.

It was evening. The sun fairy had already descended into the bosom of the Kungsör meadows,
but a dark red and purple shimmer was still noticeable in the sky: it was the last garment that the

fair goddess had removed before she retired to slumber beneath the covering. Thousands of long, reddish-blue bands radiated from the glow. Many of them striped the water, and a few even streaked the articles on the steamer.

A soft hand touched Albert's shoulder. He started up from the red beams which he had been contemplating for a long time, watching how they rocked and danced on the wavy surface of the water. It was Sara, and she said in a whisper: "You go away from here now; I'll take your place, and guard both your things and mine until we come to shore with them. Go down and drink your glass of punch. But as soon as we arrive at the landing, hurry up town and get porters before the other passengers take the men away from us."

It happened that they were standing all alone in the bow, so that it would not have been necessary for Sara to resort to whispering. Albert thought that it sounded so confidential and nice, and her pretty face was so close to him during this time, that, without stopping to think, he kissed her, and went away, as she had told him to.

As if nothing had happened, Sara Videbeck, over in the bow, began industriously to attend to a number of matters of more or less importance. She put her own carpet-bags, boxes, and outer garments together. She carried also the sergeant's trunk, traveling-coat, and medium sized knapsack to the same pile. How she knew them is a question. Her observations during the day had been sufficient for her to notice about what objects he had been most concerned during his rounds on deck, the things that he had lifted, moved, arranged, and so forth, which an honest man never does to anything except his own belongings.

Albert actually went downstairs and got a glass of punch. "Mamsell, kindly let me have two glasses more, and put them on this little tray. I'll carry them myself, so that no one will be bothered." The waitress at the buffet, happy at such a mild tone of voice from a traveler who had been so severe before, hastily did as she was told. Albert took the tray, carried it upstairs with the dexterity of an experienced waiter, and went forward to offer it to his traveling companion. " Is it carolina?" she asked; "I don't drink punch."

"Oh, have a glass of punch for my sake this evening; it's going to be cool to-night. It's fine!"

"Good!" she said, after the glass had been emptied. " Albert, this is better than carolina."

"That's just what I have always maintained," answered the sergeant, and he emptied the other glass.

Now the cannon fired a salute for the city of Arboga, and the steamer put into port on the right shore, as was customary, below the Lundborg estate.

The sergeant, agile, vivacious, and in excellent humor, was the first to jump ashore. After searching awhile in the nearest thoroughfare, he found two idle Arboga men, with whom he soon came to terms. They followed him down to the steamboat with a barrow, which they secured in the neighborhood. When he came on board, Albert at first could not find the person he sought. With some amazement he looked about in the dusk for the pink head — it was not there. Finally, however, he saw Sara Videbeck on deck — wearing her hat. Although the two men were waiting for orders, he could not help standing a few moments to survey his transformed friend. To be sure, he had had a view of the same person for a few minutes that morning, but then he had seen her without interest. Now — " Is that she ? " he thought. Once warned, however, he would not take her for a young lady of the upper classes under any circumstances. But the neat white cambric hat looked very becoming on the pretty, active, and delicate head, and a few tasteful dark locks were hanging near her temples on each side, just as was right and proper. Albert indicated to the two men the direction they had to go. Sara, with an accent on the third word, said: "These are our things; be careful they are not scratched on the barrow !"

" No fear, dear madam," said one of the porters.

" If you will point out the one you are most concerned about," added the other, "we will put that one on top."

Albert smiled to himself, but he saw a rather acid and austere expression on Sara's face. They went ashore. "Where do you want to go?" asked the porter in front.

"To the hotel."

"Oh, you don't live here? Then I must say," continued the man, "that you will have to hurry in order to get accommodations for the night in the hotel, because a great many travelers have arrived."

"I'll follow with the things," remarked Sara. "You hurry ahead, Albert! We'll find our way to the hotel."

The sergeant did so. He passed through the long Arboga streets and came, after a while, to the place.

"None to be had, none to be had!" was the inn-keeper's answer to Albert's request for rooms.

"But I come from the steamer and must have accommodations."

"Well, if you came from the sun or hell itself, it would not increase the number of our rooms. Here are Baron X and Baron Y and Baron Z, who have already engaged all the rooms for themselves and families. And as for the rest of Arboga — well, look around, my dear sir. I doubt very much, though, because of the fair in — hm-m-m — great throngs of people have flocked in."

"Well, I shall be satisfied with just one single

room—I myself can sleep in some loft," he thought—"but clean and nice, no matter if it is small. Please, money is no object."

"Has your mistress any room left anywhere, Annette?" asked the host, looking into a side room. "Some deucedly pompous noblemen have quite monopolized the place, otherwise we have room enough; but they belong to the noblesse of the vicinity, therefore you see—"

"No," answered Annette, "there is none."

"But I must have a room, confound it!" said the sergeant decisively, and entered himself. "Only one bed is needed. It is impossible not to find that in a large, spacious, and beautiful hotel like this. I have been in Arboga before, and know that a long passageway on one side of the courtyard leads to thousands of rooms in here."

"Well, well, my dear sir," said a little roly-poly in a cap, the hostess of the house. "Go, Annette, to the very end of the passageway and see whether my own room can be put in order. In an emergency I suppose I must sacrifice my own rest."

Annette and the sergeant left. He found quite a nice big room, gave his approval, and returned. He had scarcely arrived at the door before he met Sara and the porters. He showed them the way up the flight of steps that led to the boarded passageway which, like a loft or arcade, extended along that floor. The walk had made Sara cheerful again and had given her the ruddiest of complexions, but her face was once more clouded over with indignation at the porter's polite request:

"You go ahead, my dear madam!"

Soon, however, she resumed her natural expression and, accompanied by Albert and Annette, entered the designated chamber, which she found excellent. Briskly and joyfully she arranged their baggage near one of the walls. The men were paid and dismissed. Annette informed them that one of the little private dining-rooms below had just been vacated, and they both went down and enjoyed a meagre supper, which they might well need, Sara Videbeck especially.

Half an hour passed. From the dining-room they went up together, and Annette walked ahead to open the door.

"I hope you will be satisfied!" said Annette. "We have nothing better on account of the numerous travelers. I'll be up directly with a light." Thereupon she made a curtsy, stepped out, and left them together alone.

The broad and beautifully made bed indicated what the polite Annette took them for. Albert, in order to remove all embarrassment instantly, said: "My dear Sara, I'll sit in a wagon below or spend the night in a hay-loft. The stupid way those poor people address you annoys me just as much as you; but it is not my fault that broad-winged barons have taken all the rooms, so that I could get but one single room, and that only after a great deal of trouble. Still I hope you will enjoy yourself here, remain undisturbed, and sleep well."

Meanwhile Sara had removed her hat and put it on a chair. She came up to her traveling companion with a friendly gesture, and answered: "Do as you wish, and sit out there wherever you like, Albert. I can well imagine that you will make a fuss about this one nice, pretty room, and think it's stupid because there is only one. If you, like me, had been born, brought up, and lived all your life in one single room, which in daytime served as a workshop and at night as a sleeping-chamber for all of us — because the rooms that were left at home we had to rent to get money — then you would n't pay so much attention to this trifle. And though you are perhaps not exactly like many others, I understand that you have been educated with various foolish ideas. Therefore, my good Albert — well, you do as you wish; but I assure you that if you remain in here instead of sitting out there in the wet and disagreeable weather overnight, I shall not mind it at all; and I wish you would look at it in the same way; by so doing it means least."

"If you remain here, I shall not mind it at all!" passed like an echo through the sergeant's soul, and a remark so crushing to his self-respect, so cruel and depressing, made him speechless.

"Albert!" she continued, going close to him and taking his hand, "do not misunderstand me, and do not wonder! With the exception of those nights, a long time ago, when papa was still living, and for the most part stayed out, but nevertheless came home once in a while and kept on brawling, fighting, alas! and swearing, up to four o'clock in the morning, I can assure you that otherwise it was so quiet at night in our workshop, where we slept, that not the smallest piece of glass was broken. I am used to that; but you go out if you wish, my dear Albert, because you attach a great deal of importance to this trifle, and I cannot change your opinion."

It was his turn to smile; he could not help it. He released her hand. "Very well," he answered, "but first of all I'll go down to engage horses for to-morrow."

"Yes, of course, you must go at once!" interposed Sara hastily; "to-morrow it will be too late to get everything in order. We must be ready early. Stay wherever you wish to-night, but take the key to our room along when you go out, so that no one else can come in by mistake, and tell the chambermaid down there that she need not bring up any candles. I can see well enough to go to bed."

Albert left. In the door he turned. There she stood in the middle of the floor and dropped a curtsy: "Good-night, Albert! We'll see each other to-morrow!"

He bowed, closed the door, and took out the key. "Incomprehensible woman!" he muttered between his teeth. "Good-night! We shall not see each other until to-morrow morning! Is that an invitation to come back to-night? Her first reference seemed to incline in that direction. I'll go and make a round of the yard."

Down there he gave the order for the horses, and told Annette that no candles were needed, but that coffee should be carried in at exactly six o'clock in the morning. Then he roamed about in the yard to find a vehicle to sleep in. But none was to be had. To be sure, he could see through cracks in the shed some upright carriage poles, indicating that there was a supply of various elegant carriages, but they were locked in. He went down the sloping courtyard. It looked as if it would be a rainy night. He came to the stable and knocked on the door. "Go to the devil," growled an intoxicated stableman inside.

"That's a deucedly respectable innkeeper to shut up all his sheds, doors, and lofts as early as this. Prosit, sergeant, here you are in for some fun, and you are cut off from all humanity. I'll go up for a minute and see how Sara puts up with it and how she receives me. Then I'll come down here again to enforce obedience from this confounded, 'go-to-the-devil' stableman."

He was driven to this decision by curiosity; and

yet he walked back and forth several times upon
the rough, abominably paved courtyard, where he
often stubbed his toe, and talked to himself. "She
said 'Good-night,' that's true, but I noticed that
her voice trembled a little at that moment, sweetly
and incomprehensibly, as if from the inner recesses
of her heart. That may be interpreted according to
one's pleasure, as a parting adieu does not necessarily signify a complete indifference or a definite
good-night. It may be just the opposite. I have
a good mind to put her to the test, torment her,
and not go up. 'We'll see each other to-morrow!'
—therefore not to-night? But before that, however,
it was left to my own choice to determine which I
wanted to do. I will test her: I'll go up for a minute
or half a minute."

He walked slowly up the stairway, down the
long passageway, put the key carefully in the lock,
turned it, and stepped in. Here all was quiet. He
approached in the dimness. Sara's clothes lay neatly
on a chair, taken off, and folded. What about herself? He stretched his head forward to see. She was
already asleep with her face turned toward the wall.

Albert's first feeling was a fresh ecstasy, for, not
being a poet and still less a religious dreamer, but
just a plain non-commissioned officer, he was irresistibly impressed by such a wonderful and simple
freedom, such pure and unfeigned virtue. She—
without knowing whether, after all, he might not

return, which he now actually did — had serenely and sanely gone to bed and fallen asleep immediately, without inner revolt, without fears, without wrangling, and without ceremony.

But Albert's next thought was not so pleasant. He concluded then that she had been quite positively in full and dead earnest when she said that it would be of absolutely no concern to her if he stayed inside. Consequently, what was he to her? The same as a chair — a table — a doorpost — a something of that order.

Crushing! Annihilating! The most beautiful girl allows a chair to be present at her toilet without embarrassment! Altogether too flattering to enjoy the same favor!

Quiet and depressed, Albert removed his boots and coat and took a turn around the room. Since he had just been dreaming about chairs he went in search of one, and finally came upon one of these historical armchairs with enormous backs that date from the seventeenth century and are still found in old castles and small towns, where they have landed through the mighty distributing agency of the auction.

Slowly he carried his big chair up to the window, sat down, and looked out through the panes at the sky, intending to go to sleep. Alas, he could not even yawn. The chair was soft, but he felt a pricking sensation at his heart, and the whole room, as it

were, enveloped him with a dark, cold repellence.
He cast his eye toward the bed. It was shining
white on account of the hostess's clean, newly
mangled pillow-cases. In both respects, it seemed
to him that it was dead and meaningless.

He sat this way awhile and shut his eyes, so as
to be doing something. But he could see nevertheless. What did he see? A long arabesque was
unrolled before his inner eye. There appeared all
the individual happenings of the past day, and
Sara's image was constantly renewed, but so mild,
so happy. In the beginning there was the moment
in Strängnäs, when she let him call her Sara; then
when she gave him the cigar, then—and so on, and
so on. "Can it be possible, after all, that she hates
me?" he asked.

"Stupid sergeant!" he cried half aloud, and
stared up at the cornice. "Hates me? certainly not.
Does one hate a chair? Does one hate a table? Does
one hate a piece of furniture? An indifferent—a
nothing—a me!"

He listened in order to discover if, after all, she
might not be slumbering restlessly in any way. But
there was nothing of the kind discernible. "Sara
Videbeck is not one of those who dream," he sighed,
and closed his eyes again. "No doubt, after all, she
has a glass heart, hard and cold, shining but lifeless.
She certainly does not care either for hating or loving. What sort of a person is she herself, then? She

is a chair, insensible to feeling, just as she has considered me, and has told me so candidly. Virtuous? How can I call a chair virtuous? She is not at all the kind I mean, neither good nor bad. How can I call a nothing virtue or even vice?— But pardon me, sergeant, you are wrong," he went on a little while afterwards,— "she is not, as you say, a mere negation; do you remember, for example, those sparkling glances — that warm mouth?— Now and then—no, she has senses enough, you may be sure of that— but if I am the right one, ah, that's a different question. But what sort of a creature is she, then? Lewd? Heavens, no! I cannot believe that. She is an intermediate something that I should n't understand if I pondered my brains to pieces. I should like to become a poet again. Why, I am only twenty-five years old!"

"Oh," he continued, "if I could only go to sleep! To-morrow all will be well." In spite of his desire, he was now gazing most intently through the window and up toward the sky, which had become clearer, while a few stars had begun to show. He rubbed the pane of glass with his hand to remove all mist. "What is this pane in itself?" he began to meditate. "What is a pane of glass in this world? That is also an intermediate, an intermediate between inside and outside, strangely enough, because the pane itself cannot be seen, and yet it constitutes a definite boundary between the little human world

Inside and the infinitely large Outside. In the pane itself I can see nothing, but through it, nevertheless, I can see the stars of heaven. The pane is insignificant, perhaps contemptible, but for all that not exactly an inferior object, it seems to me, nor yet of any great value; in fact, it is, I think, just like myself! Oh, I should so like to inscribe my name on the pane! I have only a piece of flint in my vest pocket. I have a good mind to find out if she told the truth when she insisted that glass could not be cut with it."

He took up his flint and tried it. Either the flint was too dull, or he was afraid of making a noise by greater exertion; in a word, he could make no mark. Then he sank down in his chair with a heavy heart, and rested his head against the back. "You are without a diamond, Albert! Close your eyes and go to sleep and modify your pretensions!" The scene before his inner eye grew dimmer and dimmer, and the forms inside gradually more dull and gray. His pulse beat quickly; his heart worked very slowly and sluggishly. The universe became rather uninteresting. He fell asleep.

Chapter V

" 'Oh, there will remain very, very much for which
we shall thank each other heartily, I think, much
that no money can repay.' "

THE next morning there was a gentle knock
on the door. Albert started in his chair, and
the bed coverlet yonder was seen to stir slightly,
too. The key had been left unintentionally in the
lock outside. The latch was carefully lifted, the
door opened, and in stepped Annette with a coffee
tray

" Pardon me, my dear sir and madam, for being
late with the coffee!" she said, fluent and officious,
as waitresses sometimes are in small towns. " I see
you are already up, sir. I beg your pardon! I know
that travelers always prefer to have their coffee in
bed, but Heaven knows how it happened this morning, it is already half-past six; all the barons kept us
busy last night for a long time, before everything
was fixed to please them. I certainly hope it may
taste good to you and be clear!"

Sara raised her head and seated herself against
the pillow. Annette went over to the bed, made
a curtsy, offered her refreshments, and turned that
side of the cake-basket where the nicest rusk lay
glistening toward the "dear madam" for her to
help herself.

Meanwhile Albert had put on his boots. A
hardly perceptible nod from Sara's head constituted

a quiet good-morning. This slight smile from her new-awakened, happy countenance was for him a refreshing aurora. He thought he noticed that she was beckoning to him; he went over and sat on the broad side of the bed, whereby the part that had been unused during the night was pressed down. Now Annette served him his coffee. He took some, and it tasted good.

"Would you like some more?" she asked officiously in the door.

"Why not?" said Albert.

She went out.

After a moment's embarrassment, he remarked: "My dear Sara, I realize that you are annoyed, and rightly so, at the false titles that people give you and me; but during the journey we shall be spared many troublesome explanations and stupidities if we just let things remain as circumstances have started them—or—"

"I have realized the same thing," she answered, "and I am not vexed. I should not have wanted to circulate a lie for anything, but now that it has given birth to itself, then—and—Albert, I am very glad that you did not misunderstand me a moment ago or take it amiss, when I beckoned you to come over here and press down that part of the bed—this is a terribly wide and fine bed, I have slept like a queen—otherwise, she would have thought we were queer people."

Albert put on his coat, approached the door, and said: "I'll go and see that they hitch up."

He did so. The horses he had ordered were ready, and also the wagon with the bottom full of hay and straw and two seats consisting of ordinary hard country chairs. "She doesn't like these country things, I have heard that; the innkeeper must find me a seat with a cushion," he said to himself.

He went away, and, after a few minutes' parleying, he obtained one. It was fastened securely over the forepart of the wagon with a halter strap. "But," Albert reflected again, "it shakes cursedly here right over the axle between the front wheels. It is better to have the postboy sit here and drive, and then we can sit farther back between the axles. Otherwise I like best to sit in front and drive, but God only knows whether she likes to have the horses' tails so close, almost on her feet. Especially when you go down hill, and the horses hold back, you have them way up on your knee. Such things amuse me, but I am sure that she will not care for any such rural pleasures. I'll go up and inquire where she wants to sit."

It may be that here the sergeant's polite thoughtfulness bordered on childishness. But anyhow he ran up the stairs quickly and gleefully, reached the door, unlocked it, and went in. Sara was already standing there, dressed and ready from top to toe, except that her hat was not yet on, and the long braid was not pinned up.

"Now a real good-morning!" she said. "We have not greeted each other yet. I have seen through the window that the wagon is already waiting. But"— she added in a mild, very slow, and slightly faltering voice—"you fared pretty badly for my sake last night, did n't you?"

Her whole person, as she stood there, radiated profound gratitude combined with the pleasure of an unlimited confidence in him; and yet there was mixed with that expression not a little feminine jocosity.

Albert did not answer. But it was impossible for him at that moment not to do what he did. He suddenly took her in his arms and kissed her.

The next moment Sara Videbeck went over to survey their baggage and consider how all should be placed in the vehicle to be carried most securely. When Albert stood in the doorway, ready to fetch the postboy who was to carry down their luggage, she called him back and said:

"I have considered something. It is best that you alone make the entries in the hotel registers during the journey and pay for the post conveyances, because postboys can very seldom add, and they make me so angry, when I have to help them, that I lose my temper. But here is my portion of the fare from here to Mariestad: one horse for me for ninety-three miles at a shilling a mile makes seven and a half rix-dollars; carriage toll, two shillings; horse-and-team conveyance from the cities of Arboga and Örebro (those are the only cities we pass through) and night accommodations makes altogether eleven rix-dollars and threepence. Here you are! I don't think I have figured wrong, because I am used to it and know how. You count it yourself!"

Humiliated and with drooping head, the sergeant did not answer, but neither did he raise his .hand to receive the silver coins that were rolling out of the purse.

"My dear Albert," she remarked sorrowfully, "perhaps I have been mistaken, and you are not going so far as Mariestad. I thought I heard you say sometime yesterday that you were going to the Vadsbo district and as far down as Mariestad. I figured out our joint expenses for teams as far as that. If I have been wrong, then tell me—"

"It was not that I was thinking about," he answered. "But I do not deny that it would have pleased me to pay for all the cursed teams myself for the time being and out of my money, for I am not exactly ready for the debtor's prison, and then, when I could no longer ride in your company, we could have settled the matter between us afterwards—and—"

Sara stared at him. "Oh, is that it?" she said

finally and cast a half-sorrowful glance a little to
one side. "No, Albert, don't talk such nonsense!
All settlements afterwards are difficult for people
who like each other. You would be just as embarrassed. In fact, I should feel on pins and needles for
fear that in the end I might not be allowed to pay
it after all. To be indebted like that is unbearable."

"But good Lord, Sara, are mutual services then
— is — yes — gratitude between human hearts such
an unbearable thing?"

"Gratitude — Albert!" — her eyes were raised
now in a strangely wonderful manner — "there.
are debts that can never be paid; then gratitude is
sweet, and to be externally indebted to any one is
sweet. Let some one else be indebted for carriage
fares, money for food, rent, and careless extrava-
gances — not I. Oh, of course, if I had no money,
I should have to put up with circumstances and
accept some; be put to shame; blush, and express
gratitude; weep, and express thanks. In order to
avoid that, I intend never to be idle, and I expect
to earn money as long as possible. Don't speak
about it, take the money here in my hand, Albert,
and be a man — Oh, there will remain very, very
much for which we shall thank each other heartily,
I think, much that no money can repay."

The tear that hung suspended and sparkled from
the ends of her long, dark eyelashes while she was
speaking did not fall; it withdrew gradually back

into the eye. Accordingly, without weeping, the lustre of her eye was intensified, and it glistened with a celestial light.

Albert began to comprehend that it was not dishonorable at all to receive that money. He took it; in fact, he even went so far as to count it very carefully, as if he had taken it from a shopkeeper's hand. He found the sum correct and endeavored to utter in a very cold and strong tone: "Your account is correct, Sara."

She understood the victory he had won over himself and rewarded him with a peculiar nod. "I knew that," she said, "but it does no harm for two to add; then it will always be done better." Now she grasped her long braid of hair, coiled it neatly beneath her comb in the back, put on her hat, and walked toward the door.

The sergeant forgot to ask about the position of the seats. They went down into the courtyard and told the postboy to go up after the baggage. He left and came down with one thing after another, all of which Sara arranged in the long vehicle, while Albert went to the hotel-keeper, paid the bill, and made an entry in the register.

"I suppose I ought to see your passport," said the host, "but for people of your kind it is not really necessary."

"Why, certainly, look at it, if you want." Albert unfolded his pass before the eyes of mine host.

He began to read it. " Serg — serg — yes, that is all right. To be sure your wife is not mentioned here, but that makes no difference. It is altogether satisfactory."

" Yes, my dear host," remarked Albert, " to tell the truth, when I secured my pass I intended to travel alone. But you know one often changes one's mind, and so I took her along afterwards, although I did n't want to bother the police to make out a new pass."

" Of course, that goes without saying. What difference does it make? We don't question respectable people who travel decently and pay their bills about their passports. A pleasant journey to you, sergeant! I hope you will be satisfied with the horses. They are my own."

" Oh, is that so, sir! Well, then I may pay for the team at once as far as Fellingsbro, so that will be settled."

" Oh, no, it's not necessary; although it might be just as well: the postboy is given to drinking."

" Here you are — eight miles — and here is a little over for — Where did Annette go? Kindly take this for her!"

" Thank you very much. Have a glass on me, sergeant, if I may offer it! It will do no harm so early in the morning. Say, may I not bring out a glass and offer your wife? I have some fine malaga."

"I am afraid that Sara will not care for any so early."

"She'll have to get used to it, sergeant. Here's to you! I wager that your wife is from Västergötland. It's an excellent choice you have made, sergeant. Now I only hope the country wagon will be satisfactory and not shake you too much; but when you have no conveyance of your own, you have to be satisfied. I married a girl from Västergötland myself; that's where you find the best people. I am related to some one, I am sorry to say, who is related to Hörstadius himself. I have seen you before, sergeant — tall, handsome, and strapping fellow! And I hope I shall have the pleasure again — on the journey back — good-by — good-by!"

The sergeant could not refuse to drink; but the innkeeper's almost paternal graciousness and intimacy offended him a little and reminded him distinctly of his own status as a non-commissioned officer

Out in the courtyard he saw Sara already sitting in the wagon.

The innkeeper followed with his glass on the tray. "Permit me! Permit me!" he said, smiling.

But Sara turned away her head and remarked with mortification and in an undertone, "I have no time to spare for such things — especially in the morning."

Albert felt rebuked, but said nothing. Taking the

reins and whip, he mounted the wagon. He drove out through the hotel gate, and in his distraction came near striking it.

"Oh, look out! Look out — this won't do!" she cried.

The sergeant was mortified, because he boasted of being a good driver. He jerked the reins and gave the horses a crack with the whip, and off they went through the gate and over the Arboga road toward the western toll-gate like a whirlwind. Meanwhile the wagon was, of course, shaking and jolting up and down.

"Drive carefully, sir," cautioned the man who sat in the seat behind, as he half rose.

"Mind your own business, you fool; sit down and keep your mouth shut!" growled the sergeant.

They were now on the main highway, which was level and in good condition and permitted a tolerably rapid speed without jolting. The postboy kept quiet and went to sleep, the more peacefully as the horses were not his own. Sara had been sitting a bit stunned ever since they left the gate, and an apprehensive glance now and then to the right constituted an attempt to find out whether Albert was actually angry.

When the sergeant was driving horses he was generally so occupied with this pastime that he neither saw nor listened to anything else. For a half-hour, a whole hour, not a word was uttered.

Sara said once, "It is dusty!" This truth was irre-futable and consequently required no further comment.

After a time Sara spoke again. "It is terribly dusty! I believe I'll take off my hat."

Although the sergeant, who meanwhile had regained his temper fairly well, did not answer the remark, he asked, nevertheless, "Perhaps you would prefer to sit in the back seat? I notice that the black horse is constantly whipping your shoes with his long, untrimmed tail."

"I have nothing against that; he whisks off the dust."

"Well, all right. Then perhaps you don't care to sit in the back seat?"

"Beside the postboy? Have you not room to drive here in the front seat as it is?"

"Oh, yes, but the postboy could sit here and drive, and we could sit in the back seat; it would n't shake you so much, Sara."

"I can't say that it shakes very much. It was worse on the streets of Arboga."

"But if you should take off your hat on account of the dust, as you say, what good would it do? That would not make the dust any less."

"No, but a white cambric hat that is dusty must be washed, and that is a great deal of trouble, for it must be cleaned in the lake itself with a brush. On the other hand, the dust will come off a silk handkerchief by slapping it against your hand a couple of times."

"Well if you wish to change your headgear, I'll stop at once and we'll get out."

"Suppose I should put up the umbrella and hold that against the dust?"

"Dust does not act like rain," interrupted the sergeant, "which falls only on the top of the umbrella. Dust comes up underneath and, what is more, right around your head; I don't like an umbrella in fair weather."

Sara was silent. They drove on for a quarter of an hour without conversation. At this point the post-boy woke up and caused a terrible commotion in the back part of the wagon.

"What is he doing with our things?" cried Sara, as she turned her head. Albert held in the horses and looked back; the man had only turned over on his left side to try to take a nap in that position.

Here Albert got rid of his gloom, laughed at the grotesque position that the Arboga sleeper had assumed beneath his turned-down hat, and said: "Well, Sara Videbeck, now that we have finally stopped, we'll stay a little while; the horses can recover their wind. We have been driving fast. In the meantime you will have an opportunity to make any change you please on account of the dust."

He jumped off, went around the wagon, and

offered his hand to his companion to help her down. She stood up, but for a long time sought a foothold for the shining toe of her shoe; the hub of the wheel was full of grease. The sergeant thought she was searching too long, so he dropped her hand, seized her instead, and lifted her to the ground. "Now you will see that after riding so long you 'll have difficulty in standing."

"Oh, I feel pretty well; I think I can stand without any trouble. You certainly drive fast, Albert, especially on — You know the magistrate of Lidköping has made a law against travelers speeding through the streets."

"He is a stupid magistrate, Sara. I shall avoid going to Lidköping. But frankly, are you not thirsty in this confounded dust? I know a little spring up here on the hill. Don't you think that these environs are very pretty?"

"Are these en — en-virons? Is it far to Fellingsbro?"

"Have you, then, no love for beautiful landscapes?"

"Landscapes?" she asked, and looked about carelessly. "They are very seldom painted in a natural manner, Albert. Ever since papa's time mamma used to have a couple of landscapes hanging in the workshop at home, but I have had them carried up into the garret."

"Oh, I see. But don't you think that we have a

good view here? Just look in that direction—there, to the extreme west, lies the beautiful Frotuna, formerly the estate of Dalson, now of Count Herrmanson."

"It seems to me that we have a view whichever way we turn. Tell me, isn't this a parish? In Västergötland we always have parishes as soon as we get out of the city. Every parish has its own guild-master in shoemaking and tailoring, who may keep apprentices, but no traveling journeyman. I am glad the parishes have not come to the point yet where they keep a glazier of their own, at least not the parishes near Lidköping, so far as I know; for I have sent out assistants many times to Råda, Asaka, Goslunda, Säfvared, Linderfva, Hofby, Trassberg, and way down to Skallmeja, to put in glass for them."

Meanwhile the sergeant had gone up to the horses and talked to them, for it seemed impossible to make the pretty girl enter into any sensible conversation about the beauty of the country scenery. It should be noted in her favor, however, that the neighborhood between Arboga and Fellingsbro is not exceedingly beautiful.

"Which way did you go up to Stockholm, Sara?" he asked after a moment, when she had put away her hat in the proper box, and in place of it had tied a large, light gray, neat and glossy silk handkerchief over her head.

"Which way did I go up?" she asked.

"Yes, Sara; did n't you take the same route up to Stockholm that we are taking now? It seems to me that you are a little indifferent to the road and scenery here."

"I bought a ticket on the *Thunberg*," she answered, "and got on outside of Kålland Island when it was passing on the way from Vänersborg. Then it sailed back and forth with me continually until it came to the Riddarholm in Stockholm."

"In Arboga you seemed to know all about the inns and towns that we passed by or through on this route."

"Why, of course, I ought to know something about them, when I intended to return this way, and I took this route because I have business in Örebro and Hofva. I am to sell some looking-glass material there for Selin; that can pay for the trip. And it's an easy matter to find out about the hotels. Just look here, Albert! I have made a list of all the places, with the distances, which I took down in Warodell's store in Stockholm, according to information I received. And I went over that list by heart last night before I went to sleep."

Albert looked at her list and found a very readable woman's hand. "And this is what she lay and fixed in her memory before she went to sleep last night; just when I—" It was a crushing thought that passed through Albert. "You certainly did not busy yourself with very interesting subjects, before you went to sleep," he said aloud, with an acid glance.

"I went over all of them, both distances and names; it was not tedious. Then I figured out in my head my part of the carriage expenses, to know how much to give you in the morning before the start; it was fun — I thought of you, and was soon sound asleep."

"Yes, of course, the latter was enough to put you to sleep immediately," remarked Albert. Now the horses had rested sufficiently, and the sergeant, not in the best of humor, or at least provoked by people's ability to sleep, went over to the postboy and brought him to life by a substantial cuff. "Jack, Dog, Cur, whatever your name is, is this the way to sleep when you are coachman for travelers? Get up, and get out of that seat!"

The boy, only half awake, obedient and slavish as servants in the cities are, and astounded at the rough tone of voice, jumped out of the wagon. "What, sir?" said he.

"Well, I 'll tell you! Untie these halter straps and change the seats! Put your farmer's seat there in front, sit in it yourself, and drive. The road to Fellingsbro is now so level and good that the biggest idiot can drive. I like to drive only when it is difficult and requires skill. Now be quick about it, I tell you, you sleepy rascal! Tie this cushioned

seat in the back, right over the rear wheels, and
we'll sit in that."

The boy gradually became polite and promptly
executed the "officer's" commands. Sara Videbeck
never uttered a word during this whole conversation, but smiled slightly now and then at certain
hints that she understood.

They climbed into the wagon and seated themselves according to the new arrangement. The postboy drove now, and in so doing soon became quite
impressive. He wanted to show his cleverness; he
cracked the whip, manipulated the reins, and "away
they went like the devil himself," as the poet says.

They came to Fellingsbro presently. "Look at
those large, pretty, red brown houses!" were Sara's
first words after the long silence. She referred, apparently, to two Fellingsbro buildings that turned
their gables toward the highway. They stood sym-
metrically, with their clean, square, and spacious
yards between themselves and the garden in the
background, and were protected from the farmers
and the traffic by a fence along the road.

Albert gave no answer to her exclamation about
the houses; he alighted, settled business matters
quickly, and got horses to Glanshammar together
with an equally good carriage and seat. Again they
stepped in. The new driver, a brown and wrinkled,
but spirited old man, had to drive his horses himself, but nothing was lost by that, for he traveled

down the good road at a fairly lively pace. After a time, the road turned off to the left and south and entered the woods. The old man talked incessantly to his horses in dull, deep tones in a language that was understood by them, although it was not Swedish. However, it cannot be reproduced here. Glad at the opportunity of managing the horses alone, the old man saw nothing but the road and them.

Chapter VI

"'What! Is she capable of shuddering?' thought Albert. 'Well, God be praised! Then she is, after all — What makes you shudder, Sara?' he said aloud."

HOW I like these woods, Albert!" remarked his companion, while they rode on from Fellingsbro and entered the Käglan forest. The words were uttered in an almost caressing voice; she evidently felt that it was tiresome to go for such a long time without conversation.

The sergeant looked in her direction and thought, "After all, she has a feeling for a beautiful country!" Half appeased, he said — no, he said nothing, though he came near talking.

After a few minutes she added in a more fervent and tender voice, "Because here we are shaded from the sun and escape the dust!"

"Oh — nothing more than that!" meditated the sergeant, and remained silent.

Sara Videbeck pulled off her gloves, because her fingers were perspiring. She folded them together and put them inside her capote. Then she began to wave her two white, chubby, dimpled hands up and down in the air to cool them.

After a time, as if he had been aroused from his thoughts, Albert said mildly, but mysteriously: "Tell me, my dear, good Sara, do you never happen to dream at night?"

"Yes, indeed I do!"

"But I presume that it was a long time ago, was it not? Perhaps you have never dreamed since you were a little child?"

"I? I had a dream last night in Arboga."

"Ah!— Well, won't you tell me what it was?"

Sara kept her hands still; she let them lie in her lap, clasped together. "I can't tell you my dream," she said in a low voice, "but it was a very nice dream."

Albert remarked, "As far as I am concerned, I did n't dream after I had gone to sleep, but I certainly did before that."

"Oh — I can never believe that. Although," she interrupted herself, "every one dreams in his own way, and I suppose that is best."

The sergeant took one of her hands. "When you were dreaming last night, did you also have both your hands folded this way?"

"I don't remember where I had my hands — though I think I do remember after all," she added quietly, almost fervently.

"I 'll bet you did not dream you were in a forest, at any rate, and not that you were in the country either !"

"Nor on the lake, Albert! No, I dreamed I was in a small, small room with flowered wall-paper, and I was grinding chalk—"

"Pshaw!"

"And—still, Albert—I may as well tell you," she continued in the same tone without noticing the quivering of his nose, "I dreamed a great deal about you."

"I suppose I was grinding chalk, too!"

She looked up at him with large, glowing eyes, but lowered them as if dazed. Imperceptibly she suppressed the tears that were beginning to form and, recovering, said, "I understand very well, it's because you are an officer. I was hoping you were more of a non-commissioned officer than you really are."

This language was pure Greek to the sergeant, and the wondering glance he gave the girl told her she had uttered riddles. She withdrew her hand from his.

"That's the way with dreams," she said, apparently to herself, "and when we wake up it's entirely different. Therefore every one should be free and live his own life in his own way and not spoil things for another. People can be good friends just the same, and that is the best way. It is pleasantest when all goes well and one does not trouble one's neighbor."

Albert shook his head. "She is still dreaming," he thought.

But she continued, "I suppose God knows what He wants people to be, but I certainly don't. It is best, however, to live as God intended when He made us."

These generalities seemed so ridiculous in the
sergeant's ears that he came near laughing aloud, but
out of respect for the expression on the girl's face,
which was very thoughtful, he refrained and tried
to pursue his own line of thought.

"There is one bit of information you must give
me, Sara Videbeck," interposed the sergeant. "Your
mother lived an unhappy life with your father; I
gathered that from what you told me yesterday.
But you must not therefore think all evil comes
from men—"

"I know that well enough," she answered. "Why,
I know the family of the master turner, Stenberg.
His wife is such a quarrelsome hussy that the man
is in danger of losing his life on account of her. And
it isn't much better at Sederbom's, where the
wife is a bit simple-minded, and the man is frantic
from grief. And there are the Spolanders—and
the Zakrissons. It is the same everywhere, if one
only comes close enough to them to see them in
their cages. They never stop until each has made
an utter wretch of the other. I can never approve
of that."

"Did your father, Sara, treat your mother badly
at first?"

"God only knows. I was not born then and did
not see them in the beginning. But I think my
mother too, poor thing, had her faults, although
she tried to improve. I am sure she was always

respectable, but nevertheless wasteful and hard to get along with. So far as I can judge, her manner was never very gracious nor particularly pleasant. And so father, who had his own peculiarities, gradually became one of those—and thoroughly wicked and finally mad—ugh!"

"This is getting too distressing, Sara dear. Let's forget Lidköping; we have not got there yet. Do you know the name of these woods?"

"Yes, I think God will forgive me for being what He has made me. That is, when I do as well as I can, of course. But it is unnecessary for me to torture another into the nethermost hell or for another to drive me into it. I don't care what the name of these woods is, Albert, but I know that God has made the stars and the whole heavenly Host. All that is beautiful and good on earth has been created by God, and Christ has come for our salvation. Although I am not a Dissenter, I can well understand that Christ has nothing against the people who love each other and thus fulfill the first commandment. But when it is carried out in such a way that they make devils and madmen out of each other, He cannot approve of it Himself. People have invented so much nonsense to cause each other's misery, and worst of all, they imagine that it is for their benefit. So far as you are concerned, Albert, you are younger as a man than I am as a woman, though you may well be a year or two older in actual age. For that reason, you are not so wise as I am, though you may be familiar with other things that are more beautiful and pleasant. Still you must not think that I am unhappy; I am as free and bold as a bird, and I assure you I intend to keep my wings. If you can fly too, well and good, but if you are only a babbler, you might just as well say so at once."

Long and eloquent pause.

"I have seen that you can become offended and angry," continued the glazier's daughter. "I have no objection to that, provided your anger is at something worth while. Although," she added in a lower voice, "it is impossible to calculate or predict what will be the cause. I have observed and experienced that sufficiently. What will merely scratch the nail of one person may penetrate to the very bottom of the heart of another and burn him up like poison. I presume God knows best how He wants His people, but I certainly don't understand it."

The sergeant suddenly felt twenty years older than a little while before, and said, "Sara, I will tell you what my circumstances and feelings have been. I am not an official, and when it comes to domestic affairs you probably don't hold rank in very high esteem anyway, judging from your account of both your father and other guildmasters in Lidköping. But neither am I an officer, which in your language means that I am neither an idler

nor a babbler, at least not much of one. In short,
I am a non-commissioned officer pure and simple.
I cannot remember now exactly what made me like
you so much yesterday, and I am afraid that if I
were to tell you it would sound like nothing at all
to you. You—with your lively way of talking and
your love of moralizing—have the characteristics
of the Västergötland border as much as any girl can
have, but I am such a queer chap myself that I am
none the less fond of you on that account. Now, then,
you ought to ask me what sort of person I am, and
where I was born. You have not asked me about
that, and I must confess that your indifference has
offended me a little. However, we have long ago
ceased to talk of minor wounds; so I wish to tell
you plainly that though I have no large wings with
which to fly, I am not entirely without down. My
service for the crown is insignificant, but it gives
me the right to wear a uniform, and in the drills I
have learned how to carry myself. That is what a
man needs most of all, and with that—unless he
is a stupid, helpless cuss through and through—
he can climb as far as he likes in the world. For any
one who wants to can easily acquire knowledge.
Manners and customs are more difficult, and for an
example I need not go any further than to yourself, Sara. You have not had a chance, I think, to
learn much of the world during your apprenticeship
in the workshop, but still it isn't saying too much

when I tell you that I have never seen any girl with a finer bearing than you. I have seen a good many girls and been in a good many places, so you may depend upon my judgment. But, coming back to my own prospects, I am now on my way to the Vadsbo district, and afterwards I am going down as far as Gräfsnäs, Sollebrunn, and Koberg. I take a kind of business trip annually — both for purchases and inspection — well, I can't explain it any more thoroughly — to certain estates and properties that belong to the S. family, to which I am distantly — very distantly, Sara — related. From that I draw a certain amount of income, besides the pleasure of looking around. I have never wronged any one and never intend to as long as I live. Beyond that my ambition does not go. Still, if after a few years I shall have saved a little, it may happen that I shall buy a little place in Timmelhed over toward Ulricehamn, where I have acquaintances. I don't want to persuade you to go there, since you seem to shun the country — just as I have no particular love for small towns except as a traveler, and generally get out of them as soon as I can. As for yourself, you are happy and kind when conditions are in any way favorable, and that is at least one point which we have in common; there are probably more, if we only find them out. Whether you wear a silk wimple or a hat, I like you just the same. I have noticed that you write a good legible hand.

And finally, I am fond of planting flowers in the spring and summer—"

"In pots?"

"The devil, no, in the open ground, or at most in hothouses, if the plants are of the kind that cannot stand the cold earth. Perhaps some in pots also to have in the windows!"

"White stock—gillyflowers?"

"Exactly, they are very nice and fragrant in a room. In that case—"

"Yes, in that case the windows must have panes of pure, absolutely white glass, Albert, because greenish, coarse glass, which some poor townsmen have to be satisfied with, is such a contrast to the beautiful flowers that it is better not to have any in your windows. Otherwise I like lavender very much, because it has flowers of a grayish-blue color, which is more suitable for rooms where one has to live on a small income. Oh, Albert, you ought to see my little room— I have gillyflowers! But of course, you are going only as far as Mariestad, and then I shall have to ride alone on the dreary, sandy coast between Mariestad and Lidköping— Oh, it's such a bad and ugly road! I get frightened when I think of the journey I have to take there."

"Why should I stop at Mariestad? That is not definitely decided yet. Neither does the ugly road commence immediately on the other side of Mariestad, as you say. We pass the beautiful Kinnekulle

between Mariestad and Lidköping, besides many'
other places."

"Well, it may be that Kinnekulle is there somewhere, but it is certainly flat in those parishes. I
remember it, because I once rode from Lidköping
to Mariestad. It would be a trifling matter anyway
whether it were flat or not, but I shudder·at the
thought that—"

"What! Is she capable of shuddering?" thought
Albert. "Well, God be praised! Then she is, after
all — What makes you shudder, Sara?" he said
aloud.

"Well, I suppose I can tell you, even if it
sounds childish. I think it tedious to ride in a
farmer's cart with a peasant beside me. That's why
I seldom attend to business myself in the neigh-
boring districts, but always send the journeyman
or one of the more reliable apprentices, although I
have suffered great losses that way ; but you can't
do everything."

"What? For heaven's sake, have you suffered
great losses?"

"Yes, indeed. I don't suppose there is any one
in Lidköping for whom careless boys have smashed
more glass before it could be put in. But that mischief can be endured, it does n't go to one's heart.
Now I shall see how my poor mother feels when I
arrive."

"Perhaps she will die soon, and, as you said, it

will probably be the best thing for her. Then you
will be alone in the house. But to return to our journey, what will you give me if I go with you, not
only to Mariestad but way down to Lidköping?"

"Ah!" This little exclamation of joy was invol-
untary; still Sara recovered herself immediately,
looked at her traveling companion, and said, "First
of all, you shall receive my share of the expenses—"

"Of course."

"And—if you don't mind, you shall have a
gillyflower spray, in a new box, for which I have
cut the glass myself, lined it with gilt paper, and
glued the sides together."

"Even with that I am not entirely satisfied. Oh
well, we shall think of something on the way; we
still have many miles before that," he said.

"And perhaps," she interrupted with a peculiar
and rather pretty accent, "you will be seriously
angry with me even before we get to Mariestad. In
that case, we separate — even there."

The two parts of the sergeant's dark, neat, and
well-formed mustache were raised on his upper lip.
From this it is highly probable that he intended
to raise the lip itself, open his mouth, speak, and
perhaps say something more about his recompense
for the trouble of going way down to Lidköping.
But Sara had hardly finished the last words when
the horses shied, Heaven knows from what bush
beside the way; the tanned and wrinkled old

driver, who had been just as busy talking to his
colts as the travelers had been talking to each other,
had let the reins hang too slack, so that in the excitement he could n't hold the horses in, and they
began to gallop and run away. Horses from the
Närike province are of excellent breed and well
fed; they have fire, courage, and spirit. Consequently Albert had to get up hastily and stand in
his seat; he jerked the reins out of the old man's
hands and pulled so roughly that the two fallow
steeds had to bend their necks like high crossbows,
snort, and put their noses to their breasts. Therefore the running away came to nought, but off they
flew so that the axle bearings could easily have
taken fire.

The sergeant's hair was flying about the collar of
his doublet. Now he felt as though he were going
backward in time and were at least twenty years
younger than a moment ago. He glanced down at
his side; Sara did not seem nervous at all during
this wild ride, and this pleased Albert more profoundly than the historian is able to describe. Albert thought, " Here is still another point in which
she and I agree. Perhaps sometime I may find yet
another "

Although it is not impossible for an historian to
follow all occurrences, yet it would not do for him
to relate everything, important and unimportant,
both what was said and what was not said, what

happened and what did not happen — how often
the hat was exchanged for the kerchief and vice
versa! To be brief, the travelers arrived in Glanshammar, arrived in Örebro, arrived in Kumla, and
arrived in other places farther on.

Though the horses came near running away on
the Glanshammar road, the journey afterward did
not progress so rapidly, on the whole, as Albert
and Sara had first calculated. Because, truly, does it
not seem a good deal to have four night lodgings
between Arboga and Mariestad? And yet we must
conclude that this was the case, for they never appeared in Mariestad until Tuesday; and they had left
Stockholm on Thursday, as noted in the beginning.
Consequently, it made six days in all, of which one
was spent on Lake Maelar and the rest on land.

In all probability the delay was occasioned in
part by the fact that when they arose one morning
in Bodárna, where they spent a night, Sara was not
entirely well. She had never before experienced
so much agitation, and her eyes, though they now
seemed more brilliant than ever and were sparkling and full of the deepest fervor when she looked
at Albert, still gave evidence that she had scarcely
slept half the night. The girl who came in with the
coffee at half-past six was consequently very welcome. An excellent beverage the first thing in the
morning! But this again is no doubt too private to
mention.

Accordingly it is best to get on to Mariestad at once. It cannot be helped that the journey took six days.

Mariestad enjoys the well-deserved reputation of being one of the most beautifully located small cities in Sweden. Who but will remember the open, extensive view over Lake Vänern, especially from the church grounds! There stands the large church itself on an elevation, where it arrests the eye before one reaches the town and diverts it to the right, away from the leafy avenue in which one is driving. Finally, when one has entered the city and proceeded down the other side of the market-place, there lies the long, floating bridge, swimming idyllic on the broad, clear waters of the Lida River. And across the bridge is the beautiful Marieholm, the residence of the governor, which, though not very tall, is made all the more charming by an abundance of trees in the surrounding landscape. Memories of excellent paternal rulers of the county seem interwoven as it were with the soft branches and fluttering leaves of the maple, birch, and hazel that bend in the evening breeze.

Who but will remember all this? Yet the remembrance depends, after all, upon whether you have been in Mariestad, for it will do little good merely to hear some one talk about it; you must see the mild, inviting outlet of the Lida with your own eyes.

Albert and his companion arrived there one heavenly evening in July. Some circumstantiality must be permitted in the story in certain places, and our narrating what follows will and ought therefore to be excused.

After they had reached the market-place upon their arrival, they did not drive straight ahead, down toward the Marieholm bridge, but turned off to the right on a little street that continues to Lake Vänern itself. About half-way down this street stood the house that received the tired travelers.

They dismounted here and had the baggage carried in, and all went well. But afterwards Albert suggested that they take a walk through the town, while the evening was yet so clear and beautiful.

Of late, ever since they had left Bodarna, Sara had been more silent, not exactly solemn — that word is not suitable — but more exalted, and she did not talk so often about the business of the craft. There was no other change noticeable in her, except that the customary roguishness in her eyes had been exchanged for a certain divine kindness and consideration for almost everything that Albert wanted.

Without saying a word against it, she let him take her arm, and went with him wherever he would lead her. He had no plan for his promenade, and so it came about most naturally that they passed over the market-place down to the floating bridge,

stopped in the centre of it, and examined the Lida
River.

As they stood here and looked northward, they
had a boundless view over the clear, watered canvas
of the Vänern. They were unable to detect where
and how the lake met the reddening firmament,
for the two seemed fused into one.

"So this is the Lida!" she remarked with a little
shaking of her head. "In exactly the same way the
Lida flows through our city, and from its bridge
we have just as fine—fine—fine a view as here!
Oh, Albert, Albert! Right here I remember the moment when my mother and I stood on the bridge
over the Lida—and she hurled—the ring away—
far—far—out."

Albert suddenly shuddered, took her by the
arm, and walked away from the bridge, although
she was loath to go. When they had got up town
again, they turned to where the church stood. The
churchyard, surrounded by a low stone wall and
covered with trees in various groups, is so close to
the Vänern that the lake appears to be underneath,
and the gray, tall, imposing church itself towers
above you.

Sara suggested sitting down on a gravestone.
Albert sat beside her. "You are so quiet, my good,
beloved Sara; are you tired?" She did not even
answer these words of his; but he followed her eyes
and noticed that for a long time she sat with an

almost dreamy look—he had never seen her that way before—watching two pretty children, who were playing a short distance away on the grass; they were boisterously merry and struck each other in the face with gillyflowers:

The children looked neither poor nor rich, but unusually handsome. Albert beckoned them over to please Sara. They came bareheaded with long curls. Sara suppressed with difficulty a glistening tear, remained silent, but fondled them about the head and neck. Albert said, "Just think, Sara, suppose those pretty children were without parents!"

"They cannot be without father and mother, inasmuch as they exist."

"But if their father and mother—"

"Are dead? Well, then they are still protected by God and good people, who are always to be found. I know such a person in Lidköping who has had no children, and who has been glad to dress and help, out of his own means, several small children whose parents—Albert—"

"Have died?"

"No, worse than that; fought, ruined each other both in body and soul, and paid no attention to the children."

"You were such a child yourself at one time, Sara."

"And I am indebted for what little I am to my good Aunt Gustava, who used to visit the house of my parents by stealth. When papa died, things went a little better and more calmly at home, although mamma was already so ruined and weakened that she was worthless and could never recover; otherwise it would have been possible for her at that time to have become a real human being again. Since then I have grown up and taken the reins at home. But I feel this way, and I may give this testimony about myself, that I don't want to hurt or ruin anybody — and you, Albert, least of all. For a person to receive a right that puts her in a position to injure another to death is always horrible and always will be. God's beautiful love will certainly never make any progress on earth that way. I shall never want that power over another, and I don't intend to give it to another to be exercised over me."

Albert was silent. He patted the children on the head.

"Oh, you like children!" she exclaimed.

Without answering her, he said, "Now if the parents of these children, Sara, were unmar—"

"The children are good and beautiful; it looks as if God and man loved them."

"But if the parents were not near — did not look after them — in place of these children, Sara, we could easily imagine some that were starving, ragged, and abandoned."

"If the parents are good and sensible, she interposed mildly, "they will not fail to look after their children so long as they live; that is just as sure, I know, as that no one will tear the heart out of his own breast."

"But suppose the parents are bad and foolish?"

"Well, in that case, they are bad and foolish whether they are married or not; and they act accordingly toward their children and themselves as well as toward every other pitiable creature made by God. I have seen and considered examples enough of that, Albert."

"Yet there is one difference —"

"Yes, a big difference. I have seen that people who begin to be good and wise are apt to continue as God has created them, or else they will be kindly corrected by other people in case they make mistakes, which often happens. If they are compelled to be in bad company day and night, however, they are contaminated both in body and soul; and if they detest that company and are still obliged to live with it, then it happens very often that they become embittered, are incited to anger, and become real devils."

Albert started at this word, as always when he did not use it himself in an oath. He whispered something to himself about Dissenters.

"Think whatever you please, Albert, but I am certainly not a Dissenter; you may ask them, themselves, about it, for I give you complete freedom.

When I am talking here on the gravestone about devils, I mean those ruined, horrible human beings that can be seen in the cities — and in the country too, I think."

"That is the way man is tempted, Sara."

"Tempted? I don't believe that anybody who has the welfare of mankind at heart creates such a temptation that the great majority go down and utterly perish. And who has the right to arrange such a hellish temptation that it ends with hell itself? I don't call that temptation, it's just madness."

Albert started again and sprang up at the terrible words. Hell, madness, and devils had never entered into the conversation that he employed except, as we said before, when he swore. And in Sara's company he had never uttered an oath, at least none addressed to her, either good or bad.

To cheer himself up, he lifted the children one after the other into his arms, kissed them warmly, and glanced a little shyly down at her sitting on the gravestone. At this moment he found her looking up at him and the children, and it seemed as though she half intended to stretch out her arms toward them. He was wonderfully impressed by this picture. He was not a painter, a musician, or a poet; consequently he could not sketch or sing or express in words what impressed him in the figure of this woman sitting there and gazing upward. She was not poetical either, but the image of such pure and divine simplicity was surely worth a moment's contemplation.

"Now—now come in, Sara! It is growing late, and you may get cold. I would n't have you catch cold for a thousand worlds." He kissed the children again several times and gave them some silver coins; they ran away singing, and he took the arm of Sara Videbeck.

"Catch cold? I hope that won't happen. I am quite comfortable, Albert, though it may be that you never see me warm or with cheeks glowing."

Before they left the churchyard she turned around once, looked up at the tall, gray, majestic church-steeple back of them with a slight bow, as though she were making a curtsy as a farewell to the place —or perhaps as a token of gratitude for the pleasure she had enjoyed in the churchyard.

Albert's heart grew light again when he came out into the street. Sara also walked lightly with freedom and confidence by his side. They began to talk about the trip and various requisites. Before they realized it, they had arrived at the inn, where their things were already placed in a large, pretty, and pleasant room. It soon became so dark, however, that the woman attendant came up with a light, rolled down the window shades, and asked the guests what their pleasure was for the evening, whether they desired to eat downstairs in the public dining-room or upstairs by themselves.

"First of all, get us a bill of fare, my dear girl, then we will decide about the rest afterwards."

The girl disappeared. "Would you like to be among the people down there?" questioned Albert.

"No—and especially not to-night!" she said. "We are now in Mariestad, and there are a few matters to consider and discuss between us in case we separate here and you go southward while I turn off to the west. Let us eat up here."

The girl returned with the bill of fare. Albert indicated his choice, which corresponded with Sara's, except that she took salad with her meat, while he ordered his favorite dish of pickles. "And serve the food up here for us," he said. The waitress left and returned; all was made ready. At the end of the intimate and happy little meal the table was cleared again, and they were alone.

Chapter VII

"'But I tell you that if you want to travel around a little afterwards, I have no objection. I desire to make my own arrangements at home all alone. Forget? If you should jump up now, run out, and go to Sollebrunn to-night, would you forget me on that account?'"

WHEN they were alone, as was noted at the end of the last chapter, Sara went to their traveling-bags and began to set apart the things that belonged to Albert. "Are you going right away to-night or not until early to-morrow morning?" she said in an undertone.

"Go where?"

"I don't know where you intend to go, Albert. You have talked about turning south at Mariestad toward those large estates."

"Vadsbo district, where I had several affairs to attend to, we have now passed through for the most part and left behind us. I shall have to make that up on the return journey. To be sure, I am going to Odensåker, Sköfde, and way down to Marka and Grolanda, so the most convenient way, I dare say, would be to turn out here at Lexberg toward Kekestad and not follow the west road through Björsäter and then Lidköping. But I have business also in Gräfsnäs off toward the Sollebrunn region, and the road there goes, very conveniently, straight through Lidköping. Why could n't I take that trip now just as well?"

"Why—you say? Why, you have your own free will to take either one you wish!"

"Of course, Sara, so far as my business is concerned, I am free to do this—"

"Is there any other obstacle then? What would you like to do yourself?"

"You ask me that, Sara, and you know just as well as I that I should like to go with you to Lidköping. May I not see your little house?—your little rooms upstairs that can be let to travelers and the large room on the ground floor where you intend to keep a shop sometime, and that very soon too, perhaps, in case your mother—"

"Do you really care to see all this?"

"My dear, dear Sara, you are smiling. I really mean it. I have many trips to make here in Västergötland, back and forth during the summer, and perhaps all the year round in case I succeed in being transferred to the Västergötland Valley regiment, which depends on D'Orchimont. During these trips I must have a home somewhere—on account of my things. Couldn't you let me rent those small rooms of yours on the second floor?"

"In Lidköping? But you haven't seen those rooms yet. Wait until you see them. Never purchase, never charter what you have not first examined!"

This golden rule was framed in rhythm, and was the first of its kind the sergeant had heard from

Sara's lips, but the words fell very naturally and were recited in a sweet, almost caressing tone of voice. The two were standing near a window; they had rolled up the shade and put out the candles in order to enjoy the impressive spectacle of the evening sky before retiring.

"In those little Lidköping rooms, Sara, the wallpaper has roses on it, I dare say. And there, no doubt, you used to grind chalk sometimes in the past!" He held her in his arms, and she looked up inquiringly into his face to see whether he was making fun of the dream she had told him she had in Arboga. But now she found no irony and no satire on his lips.

"In the past?" she remarked. "That may happen many times again. I don't intend to give up my trade."

"But if I rent those rooms?"

"Then I'll attend to my affairs on the ground floor by myself."

"And then you'll never attend to anything up on my floor?"

"If you stay there for any length of time, Albert, you also will have a large number of matters to attend to for yourself and must keep things in order, according to your needs. There is a good inn nearby. You can get some one to care for your rooms very cheaply, and your washing and ironing can be done by good people who will thus make a trifle for their own support, Albert. But I want you to know that I hope to invite you down for a bit of breakfast when we have time. Perhaps you will invite me up sometime too. I shall never, never take anything that belongs to you or interfere with your mode of living — I shall merely answer you if you ask my advice, which you can take or reject, just as you please — and least of all will I ever hamper you in your work. I don't understand your business. There must be a great deal of writing and figuring, since you have to do with inspecting — well, whatever it is — Hörstadius or Selander or Silfver — or maybe it was in Koberg — but I never want to disturb you in those matters."

"Thank you, Sara, that's splendid. But may there be nothing in common between two people like — "

"We may have a great deal, a very great deal in common apart from those things, Albert. May I tell you plainly what I mean? For I have been thinking of this — during the days — "

"And I too have thought very, very much about it, you may believe; it must be our highest concern."

"And still we must be careful that our plan does not go to pieces through too great zeal. To take things lightly and wisely, just as they are, Albert, is half the battle, you know. That is the only way to take them, as we are fond of each other."

The sergeant did not understand her entirely, but stroked the beautiful hair near her forehead. "Go on, Sara, you shall speak first."

She raised her head from his breast, where it had rested for a time, meditated a little, and then said: "Since it is true that you are fond of me and I of you, we have that in common. That is a great deal, Albert. It is more than a good many have. But if we set about to have a mass of other, unnecessary things in common, then I will tell you what would happen. If you should take my little house, my means of sustenance, my property and money — insignificant enough in themselves, but of great value to me — why then I cannot deny that I might begin to be cross, because you might not know how to manage such affairs. I imagine that you hardly know yourself whether you do, since you have had no experience in looking after a house and trade. I am not certain; it is possible that my anxiety might be unjustified, and that you could manage all very well; still, the anxiety, Albert — One thing at least I can tell you, that as soon as you noticed anything of the sort in me, you would become furious. Then I should go off alone by myself and nourish my secret thoughts. One moment I should think that I was doing you wrong; the next moment it might seem as if I were right, after all, in a few things at least. In these struggles and tortures of mind and soul we should waste time which could

otherwise be spent profitably and usefully. Still the
waste of time would be the least evil. But, Albert,
I should acquire a bitter temper. You would find
me irritable, at first only occasionally, afterwards
more often. Then you would become bitter yourself. Or, if we both suppressed the unpleasant
feeling, kept it to ourselves and swallowed it, as
they say, it would turn inward instead, creep into
flesh and bone and undermine our health, and we
should waste away body and soul. No doubt, we
should have to begin to take the cure at Lund watering-place, or perhaps squander our money on
mud-baths, such as I have heard talked about in
Porla or Loka: stuff that seldom does any good
when the case is serious. Then another thing,
Albert, my complexion would soon begin to fade,
my eyes would grow dull, and I should be more
homely than I am now. You would never have the
heart to tell me that; but you would often think it.
I should have sense enough to discover it myself,
and I should go off brooding gloomily over what
you were thinking about me. Then, when you would
never tell me, I should find out for myself by
thoughts and guesses. No doubt I should lose
sleep, and that would make me still more and more
wrinkled, day by day. Yes, Albert, ugliness has no
bounds when it once commences. I have often seen
it among people. And what would you do? If you
were as good as the best of men, you would attempt

to comfort me with kind words; and whatever you might mean by them, they would sound hollow in my ears, since I should see that you lied quite a bit in order to please me. That would make matters worse and not better. You would grow tired of it too, I am sure, because, after all, you are but a human being like myself. And yet I dare say you would dislike me less on account of my losing my looks than on account of my crossness, dullness, and real wickedness of soul; and finally, perhaps, I should become foolish and stupid. That would be still more unendurable to you. Ordinary oaths and promises become mere empty words, when no man keeps what no man can keep. I am speaking about the love of a person's inmost heart; that is the only thing worth while here, and that is hopelessly lost if people become intolerable to each other. I have spoken of how I might become insufferable to you; it might well happen, also, that you would become intolerable to me. What consolation is there, then, in marriage promises? It is like a title without a position. It is like a sign-board outside a shop, and when you go inside and ask for the commodity advertised upon it, it is not to be had. What do you do then? You go out provoked and spit at the sign. Isn't that extremely pleasant? I have observed that with mortification among other people, and I don't like it. I don't want you or me to have it so. If you love me with your soul

—then I am happy and have all I want, so far as that is concerned, and beyond that I shall take care of myself entirely, be merry, satisfied, and industrious, sleep well at night, and look well during the day; I know it, and you will see. But if you do not love me—what good does anything else do, and of what use is the rest to me? To have our love last is the best and most useful thing for us; maybe it will come to an end in any case, but we ought, at least, to avoid anything that we can foresee might cause trouble and undo love instead of helping it."

" But, Sara, if we are good, sensible people, which I think we both are, we ought from the very beginning to be able—and then continue—and it seems to me that we ought not to count ourselves among the unhappy examples that you have mentioned."

"If we are good, sensible people, as I hope we are, with the help of God—why then, Albert, nothing more is necessary. Then we need only to practice our goodness and sense toward each other and toward every one else that we have anything to do with. Who can prevent it? Consider now— if we are good and rational, is it not most important that we go on being good and loving each other? That must be our main purpose, and to that end we must particularly avoid everything that tends to ruin one or make one bad and stupid and foolish. What a man continues to be is always in God's hands, and many may fall. We at least ought not to bring about conditions liable to fill the heart with poison and the brain with a misty shadow. Others may call that a trial, but I call it a wicked and unwise adventure to which people ought not, by right, to expose each other. For if God sends one a cross that cannot be avoided, it must be endured bravely, and that is a trial. But people should leave alone entanglements that may bring wretchedness; such are avoidable and should be shunned. They are not to be called trials, especially since they generally lead to hell, whither no kind Providence would want to drag those subject to it. But if you don't believe as I do, Albert, you are entirely at liberty, and —"

"At all events," interrupted the sergeant, "you are wrong, Sara, when you say that there is wickedness and unhappiness in all homes."

"In all?" she asked. "No, I have seen one or two where they lived happily, but that is not because they have been read together, which does not help matters in the other cases, but because they agree with all their soul or at least as much as is necessary, and that always helps."

"Read together? What do you mean?"

"Why, that some one has read a blessing over their heads. Dear Albert, sorceries are of no use. In this affair, as in all others, we must realize sometime that we must seek only what is really valuable and not build upon the worthless; for that breeds

not only unhappiness but, what is worse, real vice.
Because when love is gone it becomes a vice—"

"Sorceries? I like very much the beautiful prayer
which is used, for instance, when two—"

Sara looked up with a wonderful expression. "God
is my witness," she said in a scarcely audible but
very clear voice; "God knows that I love prayers.
I pray, Albert, and expect to pray, but I do not use
prayers where they avail nothing, for that is sorcery
and empty sound, if not something worse—blas-
phemy. Prayers? Oh, great God! Not the most
beautiful of prayers can change black to white or
white to black. If two stand beside each other and
even then pretend a fondness they do not feel, does
prayer convert the lie into truth? Or if they do
not stand there and lie just then, but nevertheless
promise what they may be utterly unable to keep
afterwards, can that be prevented by any prayer
read over their heads? What usually happens, when
they later fail to do what has been impossible for
them to do, is that they keep up appearances and
increase the torture and falsehood. What, may I
ask, did the poor prayer accomplish then? It certainly did not prevent matters from going that way.
When they still continue to live together, they sink
lower and lower in body and soul—yes, become
really immoral, we must admit—and finally are
unable any longer to see what is beautiful and pure
in the world or understand anything that is funda-

mentally sane about man, despite the fact that they once were blessed. Why, you see that constantly, and I call it immoral, Albert! It is surely not worth while to be called good, noble, and happy without being so! And to obtain a result it is never worth while to use any other means than those that will obtain the result—that is what I think. When I need oil for my chalk, you don't suppose I begin to read a blessing over it, do you? No, I go out and get more oil to mix with the chalk, and that helps. I never resort to sorcery, Albert, although many persons in Lidköping throw grains of salt into the oven when they have a toothache, run lead over sick folks, and stick splinters into trees. Sometimes they claim to have recovered, which might have happened anyway, though not on account of the splinters, I imagine. In the same way, those who are read together may live quite morally, but it doesn't really come from any ceremony."

"Well, the reading does no harm, at least."

"Yes, indeed it does, for when we have once read the marriage ceremony over two persons who can only be a means of destruction and misery to each other, we still claim and insist that they must live together and crush each other henceforth, just on account of that reading, which took place needlessly once. It seems to me very harmful. Likewise, I dare say, it works mischief to use prayers in vain, and in most cases a terrible injury. Oh, my God—and how prayer, which is so holy and good, avails at the right time is something I know well."

"Dear girl, when did you pray last?"

"In Arboga—Albert." She whispered this very softly, and it sounded almost as though a *my* preceded the name Albert; yet the whole expression was too magical to be retained, although for a moment it was too deeply captivating ever to be forgotten. She was silent, but immediately afterward she added: "I repeat it, Albert, if you do not believe as I do, you are free to do anything you wish with yourself and your property. Simply tell me, for in that case, I would just as soon have you go to-night or to-morrow morning and not come along to Lidköping, although God knows how much I should like to have your company on that sandy, disagreeable road."

"Merely on the road?"

Their warm glances met; but they had not looked long into each other's eyes before they gazed out through the window-pane and up toward the sky, which did not seem to have grown darker, although they had spent a long time in the twilight. Albert sat down on a chair near the window, took Sara in his lap, and now remembered beyond Bodarna that dusky night in Arboga, where he had also sat by the window-pane, and had tried in vain to inscribe his name upon it. How much had changed since then! What a new life! With what different eyes did he look upon her now, and she herself seemed to have been transported into another world. All the rough, pert, tomboyish air which had often been visible before had disappeared. She now bore the marks of a womanly citizen: the same common sense in everything as before, but a sense that was subdued in the aroma of the deepest devotion, the purest loveliness. The most wonderful thing was that, despite all, the absolute freedom she granted him to leave her if he would and when he would, instead of tempting him to desertion, made her a thousand times more amiable, gay, and delightful in his eyes. "And amiability is the only quality — the only one — that will attract genuine love. It may not come even then, perhaps, but if anything will draw it out, it is that alone," he meditated.

"What are you looking at up in the heavens, Sara?"

"I am just wondering if it is far up there."

He pressed her to his breast and answered, "We are on the road."

"Merely on the road?"

"No, we are there now — if — "

"Albert!"

"Tell me, Sara, sincerely — you were just speaking about how a person might become ill-looking through inner grief and torment of the soul, and in that you were surely right. We shall leave such things alone. But really, Sara, you could never become unattractive. That seems impossible to me——"

"In soul, Albert, you and I need never become ugly, and I think that will do. But you know very well that in body, when we become old, we——even without wasting disease——"

"What do aged features signify when a good and true spirit is reflected in the eyes and in the expression of every lineament? It is by this heaven that I am attracted and enraptured."

"I think so, too. Thank God, you are not a fool, Albert."

"And even physical features are very slow to decline, very slow, provided a good, lively, and active spirit lives within. That's my opinion, Sara."

"I have seen that in my Aunt Gustava," she interrupted.

"Let us then arrange things this way, Sara: each of us shall manage his or her own affairs. I will not let you direct mine, just as you shall not give me control over yours. We shall just have our love in common. But suppose that one of us should ever be in want, so that his own means were not enough to live on?"

"Wouldn't love be willing to help in such a case?" she demanded, continuing, "If you should get into trouble, Albert, wouldn't I give you of my resources as long as I had any and knew that you were no wretched squanderer? And if I should become very poor, it might happen that you—that you would be willing to give me something?"

"Good heavens, how you talk, Sara! When that feeling is mutual, have we not our resources in common already?"

"No, there is a vast difference. If I make you a present of money or anything else, you can do whatever you wish with it. No mischief will arise from that; it becomes yours just as what you had before. If you ask advice of me about the handling of it, I will answer you, and then afterward you may treat the advice as you think best. In that way, despite the gift, you remain free; neither will your affairs be disrupted nor your morals corrupted. Similarly, if you wish to make me a present of anything, you must make it on the same terms, as a pure and unselfish gift of love, for pleasure and service, which I may appropriate and use as I please and need. Such gifts and return gifts are an actual aid to man and not a mutual means of destruction such as the daily tangles that people are constantly getting into with one another."

"Can people never manage a household together, then?"

"Why, they may try. If the housekeeping goes well, they may continue with it, of course, just as you continue with anything else that goes well. On the other hand, if it goes wrong, it is wise to stop, just as you do with anything else that goes wrong.

But love between two persons should, first of all, be protected from and undisturbed by dangers of that sort. However well it may turn out, love should never be made to suffer from or depend upon external domestic relations. My belief is that a man and a woman should never live together, because people who are in love provoke, irritate, and finally ruin each other more quickly than those who do not care so much about each other, and therefore regard many things with indifference. But if, after all, they insist upon the unnecessary pleasure of letting two heads rule over earthly affairs that are best managed and remain least involved when they are not joined together but handled by each one separately, according to the best of his ability—then, may they at least be prudent enough to stop before their love passes away, which may easily happen! For though no glass is more beautiful than the heart's fancy, no enamel is more brittle. That I can see."

"Why, it would be better, then, if we not only lived apart, but also refrained from seeing each other too often."

"Well, you expect to travel around a great deal, don't you, Albert?" she said with a glance that was far from pained.

"I must, I cannot avoid it."

"How gladly I shall think of you when you are away! You will have a hard time to keep yourself

as handsome as the image of you in my soul when
you are absent. But you can return and each time
be doubly welcome!"

"But good heavens—"

"In that way love will last. You won't have to
see me in all kinds of dull, stupid, and disagreeable
—well, in moments when it is entirely unnecessary
to see each other. If you, too, should have such
moments, because you are a human being, Albert,
I shall also be spared seeing you then."

"But great God, Sara, I don't understand—
where will this end? May we not forget each other?"

"Those who are in daily contact and feel bored
by it forget most quickly, Albert; or, if they do
remember each other, it is with pain, just as one
remembers a felon."

"Ugh!"

"Their bodies are intimate with their souls apart.
As the Scriptures say: 'This people honoreth me
with their lips; but their heart is far from me!'"

"You surely are a Dissenter!"

"If there must be a choice, then I prefer intimate souls with bodies apart."

"But may not both be intimate?"

"Sometimes, Albert. That is now the case with
us. Still—and I want you to come with me to Lidköping. But I tell you that if you want to travel
around a little afterwards, I shall have no objection.
I desire to make my own arrangements at home all

alone. Forget? If you should start up now, run out, and go to Sollebrunn to-night, would you forget me on that account?"

"Sara, you would stand continually before me!"

"And I should see you through all my windows. Try it! Just go for the fun of it!"

"Let me linger a while."

"Forget? It is when indifference comes between people that forgetfulness slides in alongside. What do journeys signify? Highways create no distance between souls. Well, I'll admit that I don't want you to be away more than half the year."

"You breathe very lightly!"

"Forget?" she resumed after a moment's pause. "Maybe if love dies out, forgetfulness comes also; but one thing is certain: I know that happy memory in the heart is not nourished by anything that consumes love itself. Therefore——"

"Very well, I shall not see you nor visit you too often, Sara, but if I may rent your rooms and sit there at my own work, nothing in the world, not even you yourself, will be able to prevent me from painting your picture before me, not with a brush, I am not able to do that—— oh, if I only could!—— And if you should get sick, then I'll go down and sit by your bed."

"That depends on the nature of the sickness, dear Albert. I prefer to have Mary there; she understands better."

"But—great heavens—if—I was just thinking—suppose I should get sick myself?"

"That's an entirely different matter. Then I'll go up to your room and sit beside your bed day and night, if necessary. I'll close the shop and put up a notice: Out of Town. You must know there is a difference. If a man is sick—really sick, so that it isn't mere talk, if he is seriously confined to his bed—it is not unpleasant or tedious to be in attendance; I understand all about that. But a woman who is sick abed with consumption, or something similar, had better be by herself, Albert. Still, if anything should happen to me, I don't object to your staying in the town—in the house—on the upper floor. If I should—"

"God! What is the meaning of the wonderful expression in your face?"

"If on that occasion I should come near death, I should want you to come down to my room—just before I die—to me—and—because I should want this hand to be the very last that I kiss in this world . . . "

Chapter VIII

"'Look about and look happy! I should like to have the secret joy of knowing that, when you drive through the streets, every other girl might stop and say to herself: "Goodness, what a handsome officer!"'"

HISTORY and Geography, which always go hand in hand, must have come to each other's aid, so that when the former recently and suddenly withdrew, the latter began to speak as follows: "The highway between Mariestad and Lidköping extends all the way from Mariestad to Lidköping." The two travelers started on this road early the next morning, as soon as they had dipped their rusks in a couple of pretty cups of real porcelain.

The geography of Västergötland may say what it pleases about the southern shore of Lake Vänern, but one thing is certain: that if you don't look at the road that follows it, the view is not at all unpleasant to the eye. When the two travelers had arrived at Bresäter, Albert said: "Now it's a question whether we shall take that divine route near Forshamn, passing over Kinnekulle, through the northern part of Österplana, then Medelplana and Källby, which should take us to Hönsäter, Hellekis, and Råbäck—"

"Råbäck? I have heard about Råbäck! I have not been there before," replied Sara. "But why should I go there now when she is no longer there?"

"Which she?"

"An angel used to live there who has now moved to Lake Vänern."

"Mrs.—I know—I don't remember the name exactly."

"I have not seen her either," continued Sara. "But if she were still living in Råbäck I should like to go that way. She used to lend Aunt Gustava in Lidköping excellent books, and we read them together in our spare moments."

"I want to read them too!" exclaimed the sergeant.

"You shall—but—"

"And now the other road that we can take," he went on, "goes down toward Enebacken, east and south of Kinnekulle, through Skälfvum, by Husby, and so on. Which one shall we take?"

"How can I decide that? I don't know anything about it."

"But you must know, Sara, that Hellekis is one of the best places in Västergötland; it would probably be worth while to go that way."

"As you wish. If there are any big houses there, it would no doubt pay to become familiar with the place; it might be profitable sometime."

A bit disheartened, the sergeant took in the poetic sail of the conversation. He had not heard her business affairs mentioned for several days, but perceived at once that they were approaching. How

could he be displeased with her for that? Still he did
not care to have such divine estates as Hönsäter,
Hellekis, and Råbäck sacrificed as a mere goal for
the material wishes of a glazier; consequently he
decided to take the prosaic route over Enebacken,
leaving Kinnekulle to the right.

"But she was in a more exalted frame of mind,"
continued the sergeant to himself—"yes, for a
couple of days, and the subjects of her conversation,
although always alike in wisdom, did not always
savor of a journeyman in woman's attire. Poor,
good, innocent girl!" he added with a half-suppressed tear. "My dear and beloved! How wrongly
I judge you! Isn't it quite right for you to be so
rational? You will be able in an honest and excellent
way to take care of yourself and your—"

He jerked the horses as if they had been seized
by a sudden fright and he feared they would shy
to one side. He recovered and continued to himself: "All that I can save and lay by I will give
them, as a complete and free gift, just as she wants
it, without any interference on my part, unless it
be free advice about what to do with it. But, good
God, I will call them mine: I will; I must; that is
my fixed determination."

"That you shall, and it will be my heavenly joy
to hear you say so—" Albert started, alarmed, when
Sara uttered these words. Had he forgotten himself
in his dreamy speculations to such an extent that

he had talked aloud and betrayed his innermost thoughts?

"Don't be frightened, Albert, I can hear your whisperings, your most silent whisperings to yourself, because I am so constituted that I can hear."

"Great God! Who are you, then? Can you do more than others?"

"You drive so well and gallantly, Albert—I love you!"

"You love me, but you do not answer me!"

"What question am I to answer?"

"How could you, a moment ago, hear what, hesitatingly, only my soul dared imagine?"

"I love your soul, therefore I can hear the words of your soul."

"What?"

"That is to say, I understand you. I comprehend your thoughts—even what you were brooding about just before this—"

"What! About your occupation?"

"Exactly. A window-pane is not so contemptible as you think, Albert. In winter time it protects you from the cold outside and still gives you light. Most things in life that give you heat do so only without light, or if they give you light, it is seldom without cold. Only a window—notice this carefully, my Albert—gives light without allowing the cold to rush in; and it keeps the heat inside with the addition of light. That is the nature of a window, and it means more than many persons understand. For that reason you must not despise windows, nor Sara's occupation by which she has fed herself and all those in Lidköping whom she may have assisted or will assist hereafter—even you, Albert, if you get into trouble."

"No, Sara, that will never be necessary. I shall be industrious, very industrious in my occupation —for I have an occupation, too! Now, my dear, good girl, I am just beginning to feel the happiness there is in work! I will and shall earn! Work formerly sounded so paltry in my ears! I will toil! Thereby I shall not only help myself, but—all those in Lidköping that I may need to help. Occupation and industry—you, Sara, have taught me the right words!" He took her hand.

Geography is a poor thing that constantly lets itself be caught napping by History. When was it the latter resumed control? Oh, yes, on the way to Enebacken. Very well, then, take it up again there and stick to it, Geography!

Enebacken—and then we have the churches of Holmestad, Götened, and Skälfvum, and even Vetlösa a little to the left. Later one can see Husby and even the churches of Klefva up toward Kinnekulle. Farther on the view discloses Broby church, Källby church, and Skeby church—What an amazingly large number of churches!

But now there are no more. On the right, a large open body of water strikes the eye of the traveler and thrills him with delicious terror. He fears that the whole Vänern will rush in, at least as far as the hub of the wheel, and doubts not that the marshy, yellow, sandy shores upon which he is driving lay at one time beneath the waves. Lake Vänern is a fairy who has withdrawn a little. Who knows but she may suddenly and unexpectedly return and recapture her old rights. Especially in a northern storm she can be terrible.

To-day the wind was quiet and the lake smiling. Sara sat and expected to see her Lidköping at any moment, while the most delightful inner emotions were passing through her mind.

But History must be allowed to explain one thing: that is the extraordinary good fortune they had experienced in getting a four-wheeler, because otherwise most travelers who do not have their conveyances are threatened by carts, and carts are sometimes disagreeable to ride in. Consequently it was a kind Providence that directed matters here; and perhaps the nearest explanation is the one propounded by the doctors themselves—who otherwise do not concern themselves about Fate—that Nature takes an excellent and special care of woman; that Nature is almost afraid of injuring her and is respectful, solicitous, and watchful. This is a mystical but sacred thought. May man be respectfully considerate to the same degree. May we kneel before a heaven that surrounds us, unknown — misunderstood — so close to us, so good, so mysterious, forgotten and yet eternal.

The good fortune to obtain a four-wheeler came often, because when Albert saw the horses were good he did not care to ask for a driver, but drove himself. This arrangement is gratefully welcomed by the tavern-keepers when they see they have respectable travelers. And so the sergeant and Sara had been riding alone the whole time.

They had reached Lidköping. They began to ride through the main street of the city, a good, broad street, but somewhat unevenly paved. "Dear Albert, let me get off here; this is the home of my youth: I should like to walk here. You can drive, I'll walk alone."

"No, I'll get off too and walk alongside and drive."

"No, that does n't look well. And besides, Albert, I would rather you rode alone to the tavern beyond the market-place, while I go home. I want to go there alone first. I want to see how my poor mother is."

"I wish to see her also."

"No, Albert, if she is still living, she would be terrified at the sight of you. I don't want you to come."

"Great God! What do you say?"

"Because you could not help betraying yourself. You would act in such a way toward me that she would suspect your love. She would tremble at the idea that in you she was looking at her daughter's future husband. It would be difficult for me to convince her that you would never be—"

"Ah—"

"But fear nothing, my dear Albert! You shall soon come to us and examine the rooms that you intend to rent. Wait until I send for you. Now drive straight ahead. It is not difficult to find your way here in Lidköping. Without turning off, you will come right to the bridge we have talked about, over the Lida River—you know the one that—"

"Oh!"

"Well, you drive over it, but take in the view to the right and to the left, for no more beautiful river than the Lida flows through any town. A little beyond, on the same street, you will come to the market-place. No bigger market-place is found anywhere in the world. Drive straight ahead through it to the beginning of the street farthest away to the left. That street goes toward another toll-gate, from which the road runs to Gothenburg. When you come along that street, you will find a tavern at the corner of the first crossing beyond the market-place. Put up there, have our goods carried up, and engage a room for yourself for the night, or until I let you know. From home I shall send over one of the apprentices for my things; I dare say you can tell them apart."

"I don't suppose there is an S. V. on all, but I will try."

"You are absent-minded, my dear Albert. When you get to the tavern, have something to eat, refresh yourself, and don't think so much about me. You know your own things, don't you?"

"Everything that isn't yours is mine."

"But—don't be low-spirited, don't be pale! You are in a respectable town, I tell you. Take a look at the people when you drive through the city; you will observe that almost every girl here is pleasing—Lidköping is noted for that—I am one of the most insignificant. Look about and look happy! I should like to have the secret joy of knowing that when you drive through the streets, every other girl might stop and say to herself: 'Goodness, what a handsome officer!'"

The sergeant nodded a tolerably cheerful goodby to Sara, who had dismounted. He drove on, but slowly, and turned often to look at his walking companion.

"You drive too slowly," she said, beckoning; "that won't do for a man." He cracked his whip anew in the air, the horses started off quickly, and Sara Videbeck walked alone.

She turned off down a street along the river, the street that led to her home. It was not late, but already evening. Several clouds in long, ragged, and shapeless forms passed over the sky here and there; but there were no signs of rain. The sun in the west was playing with the sombre, thin, light gray cloud forms.

The pedestrian stopped near a crossing, for there were people approaching on foot, and she looked for acquaintances among them. In small towns everybody knows almost everybody else. Sara recognized them, but they were deep in conversation and quite a distance away, so they did not see her. She wondered at their gestures, pointings, and noddings. When they passed, she also moved forward and approached the next corner. Here she stopped short again, for a funeral procession came along. Respect for anything of that kind had always held her back. How much more so now, when she recognized with amazement and alarm her own journeyman dressed in black in the procession. A few of the older apprentices and other acquaintances were carrying a coffin. There was no doubt it was her mother's.

She sought to suppress the terrible emotion within her breast and her difficulty in breathing, for an improper scene on the street had to be avoided. Dressed in traveling-clothes and without anything black, she did not wish to show herself. "My mother! My mother! Shall I never see your face again?" she cried, wringing her hands and with-

drawing farther into the corner where she stood
to let the sad procession pass. She thought she
could hear the cantor softly mumble to his neighbor the words "last Sunday night."

The mourners did not notice her. When the coffin had passed the quietly weeping, hidden daughter, she felt it impossible to continue her journey
home. She saw that the procession turned toward
the church. Whether it was to be a funeral service
or a mere interment she could not know, but she
was drawn on irresistibly to follow at a distance.
As yet all was confused, ghastly, and too sudden
and surprising. To see her mother, or at least to
touch the coffin with her lips before it was lowered
into the grave, was a necessity.

"Last Sunday night?" She spelled out the words
in her thought. "Where was I then? Last Thursday I left Stockholm. If there had been no delay
— if I had not — if — we could have — I could have
been home last Sunday night. Now it is Wednesday! Where were we Sunday night? Where? In
Bodarna," she answered herself.

The location of the Lidköping church differs
from that of Mariestad, because the latter stands
on an elevation overlooking the whole city and can
be seen everywhere, whereas Lidköping's church is
tucked away in a corner of the town, in such a way,
to be sure, that it may be seen at a distance — for
it is quite a large building, after all, but not one

that attracts the eye immediately from every direction. It is not built on the very shore of Lake Vänern like the church in Mariestad, but is surrounded by a much darker and more intimate churchyard containing a much richer and denser foliage.

Sara would not come near the procession, partly because women never participated in funeral processions; the mourners in particular did not appear in public, least of all in the cemetery at the interment. But Sara simply had to go to the graveyard! It was to be a service; her eyes, strained to the utmost, must seek to follow this last journey of the beloved as long as it was possible.

She discovered with emotion that the ceremony had been entrusted to the humblest clergyman in the town. The coffin was surrounded by people who had been the workmen of the glazier's widow. They had not been accustomed to go dressed in black, and now they looked poorly fitted out in clothes that were to a large extent borrowed or at least outgrown. But all their faces, when Sara saw them pass, seemed to have pale and sunken cheeks. "Have they fared so badly during the three weeks that I have been away?" No, she hoped it meant sorrow and devotion. The coffin was already far inside the churchyard, when the daughter with tottering steps also tried to venture in.

She looked about inside. No group of people had gathered with which she could mingle or dare ap-

proach nearer to the heap of earth upon which her
staring eyes were fixed. And so she withdrew to
one side, to a tall gravestone at a distance beneath
a tree. Concealed there she could still behold her
mother's last — and only — honor. There was a faint
tolling of the smallest bell in the church, the clergyman opened his service-book, and the cantor
began his hymn.

At these sounds Sara fell down on her knees in
the grass near the solitary gravestone. The tears
streamed from her eyes, her head sank tremblingly
far down toward the flower-covered mound, and
her hands hid the lowered forehead. "My mother!
My mother!" she cried aloud, for she knew that
no mortal heard her here. But a blissful memory
thrilled her heart at that moment: "I have fulfilled
your wish, mother! I have heeded your constant
warning. Oh, wherever you are now, give me your
blessing!"

If the spirit of the deceased had now looked
around on what was taking place, it could have observed the black-dressed individuals carefully and
respectfully busying themselves about the grave,
though not with many words, for there was nothing to eulogize, of course, in the life of the glazier's widow. But here under the tree, as a source
of greater joy for heaven and earth, knelt a beautiful image of future ages and generations: here
was a picture that the spirit might look upon with

a greater, yea, with an infinite felicity. Heavenly virtue, pure morality, and true duty are often unknown, misjudged, and unnoticed qualities. Concealed and quiet stood the daughter in her prayer. No human being noticed her. A cool breeze blew over the flowers.

The verse of the hymn was short, the tolling of the bell came quickly to an end, and the words of the clergyman were limited to those of the service-book. Consequently everything passed entirely as it should; nothing was lacking, but neither was anything added. There were dark blue circles beneath the sunken eyes of the foreman. The apprentices, of healthy complexion, seized the ready shovels and began to fill in the grave.

Albert had reached his destination on the street corner, engaged a room on the second floor of the inn, and was promenading back and forth in it, now restless, curious, and waiting for a message, now dispirited, high-spirited, or low-spirited. He looked at his watch; it was seven o'clock in the evening. To engage horses at once for the next day and start off early for Sollebrunn seemed impossible just then, but at eight o'clock he found this the proper course to take. But ought he not first to take leave of—and when would it be proper to return? To be sure, these were not deliberations of the most involved kind, but he had already become accustomed to deliberate about many things together with a certain individual; he wanted to do so even now, and he felt lonesome.

His restlessness was finally concentrated in one single focus. He sat silent, stiff, and staring in his corner sofa, wondering why no message came. He heard a chambermaid close a few doors of rooms outside. He called to her with a thundering voice. She came flying. "Give me a cup of tea!" he said, and looked wild.

Accustomed to peculiar travelers, she went on her way, politely, silently, and without astonishment. Then he called her back, and she returned. "Did you hear what I asked for?" he growled.

"Yes, sir."

"Then be quick about it, while I sit here and wait!"

"You have not been waiting for me, I know that much," she said offended and went out ruffled.

"Oh, how I long for you!" he burst out, sighing to himself, without having listened to the retreating girl.

The tea came, hot and strong. Even the girl who carried it looked vexed, for any one may lose her patience, and when the sergeant put the cup to his lips, he burned himself so badly that he yelled: "Oh-h, the devil!"

"Couldn't you have waited a little with it?" he burst out. "I am not made to be scalded."

"Neither am I," answered the Lidköping girl adroitly.

"Are you crazy?"

"No, *one* is enough."

"I'll put in more sugar and cream, and then it will cool off," remarked the sergeant, who had come to his senses and regained his temper. "What time is it?"

"That's none of my business."

"You're a deuce of a girl!"

"Will you have another cup?"

"I see it is almost nine o'clock, and still there is no message. Make up my bed at once; I want to go to bed, and then I'll have something to do. Yes, give me another cup!"

"You want it in bed?"

"Pour it out and let it stand there, and I'll see. I am going out on the street to look around a little; but if any message comes, call me back. And meantime get the bed ready!"

"A queer officer!" said the girl after he had gone out. "But he is expecting a message, and I won't bother with him." She made the bed promptly and quickly. She was angry. Sheets and pillow-cases flew back and forth like the wind under her hands. The bed was ready in a trice, as he had demanded.

Truly melancholy, pale, and with his head lowered toward his breast, the sergeant returned. "Has any message come?" he asked most politely of the chambermaid, who was hurrying down the stairs.

"No, but everything is in order now." She disappeared below. He went up the stairs.

Stunned for a moment, he said nothing. He cast one more glance through the window on the street to find out whether— But nobody was to be seen.

He sat a long time near the window; but nothing happened, except that it became darker around him. "I am going to bed!" he finally said aloud, but slowly and absent-mindedly. No objection was made to this assertion. Nobody was present to dispute the least thing with him.

He undressed drowsily, lay down, and went to sleep, wrapped in the innkeeper's sheet and gray-spangled silk coverlet, expensive in itself but of no value to the sergeant.

The next morning—it was Thursday again, judging by the evening before, which had been a Wednesday evening—it happened that the sergeant woke up. No one greeted him, no one got up by his side, and no one nodded; no one came in, even, for in his affliction he had entirely forgotten to order breakfast the night before. Still he was enough of a man to get up and stand on the floor.

"Incomprehensible," he meditated.

He washed his head with cold water, dressed himself as elegantly as the cut of his uniform would allow, and finally stepped up before a large pier glass to put on the finishing touches. His cheeks had assumed a delicate complexion through their pallor; the large, dark, and now wistful eyes, the handsome, curly hair, and the whole picture in the mirror looked as if he had been promoted to an ensign. He was provoked at this, because a definite and unfathomable desire had come to him to remain for a time a non-commissioned officer. "Out upon you, weakling!" he mumbled; dark flashes of lightning gleamed from the corners of his eyes, and he hurled bold, angry glances at his adversary in the glass, which for obvious reasons were instantly repeated by the man in the mirror. Thus these two gentlemen encouraged each other, and within the hour the sergeant looked like a Swedish Achilles.

Some one came tripping along, the door opened, and the chambermaid stepped in with the announcement that a messenger had come for the things the night before, and that those rooms for rent—

"A messenger? And I have not been told of this until now!" Thunder threatened in these words. The girl hastily turned toward the door, but recovered and explained that the messenger had come so late that the "major" had long been asleep and that she would certainly not have dared—

"Where did the messenger come from?"

"From the Videbeck woman."

"Videbe—" Again a lightning glance: still he

could not deny that the right term for the intermediate which he had pondered about so much might
sound just that way. Yet he dared not pronounce
the name that way himself.

"Yes, or more correctly speaking, from that
house," continued the girl, "for the woman herself is gone at last. But the apprentices recognized
the things and carried them back to the house of
their dead mistress."

"Dead! What do you say? Heavens and earth!
Dead? No—and I was told nothing of this yesterday!"

The girl answered, amazed: "The messenger said
that those rooms to rent might be rented now and
they could be examined at eight o'clock this morning. For that reason I did n't think it worth while
to disturb you, major, before seven."

"To be examined at eight, said the errand boy?
Look here! It is quarter to eight. But—eternal
God! Dead? That's impossible! Impossible! Im-
possible!"

He rushed out and at the door asked the way
to the Videbeck house. The maid told him and
described it as well as his impatience and her astonishment would permit. He hastened off.

The morning was marvelously beautiful. The
sergeant reached one of the streets near the Lida.
The sunlight of a new day together with all the
blue, the green, the white in the air, in the trees,

and in—Oh, the sergeant should have had sense enough to behold and rejoice at so much! Surely he should have concluded from the conversations of the preceding days that it was the Videbeck mother that had died and not the daughter at all. But he was so full of thoughts that he passed on without reflection.

Finally, he saw a little red, wooden building resembling a house in Strängnäs, but in good repair. He came upon a long line of spruce twigs in the street; he felt a pang within his breast: now he had the death line to follow.

Through a board gate with a latch, he entered a spacious, newly swept yard. He went up the low, broad front doorsteps. The door itself, which was quite large, was decorated with boughs of sweet maple and birch. Garden chevril and fresh meadow-sweet exhaled their perfume from the floor of the entry. He smelled this mild fragrance, but his knees trembled, for he felt that it had the customary purpose of concealing the fumes of something dreadful.

An elderly woman came to meet him. She was neat, but dressed extremely plainly, and with a mingling of sorrow and goodness in her countenance. Again he felt a stinging pain in his heart. "That must be old Mary!" thought he. What should he say? How should he commence? Finally he stammered: "I have heard that there are rooms here to—"

"To rent? Yes, upstairs, if I may show them to you."

He went toward the stairway, but he shuddered, for if she were really dead, what in the name of God would he want with the rooms? His foot came near stumbling over the first step; he turned around toward the old servant, he wanted to ask a question, but his tongue refused to obey. In order to do something, he said: "Before I go up, let me know the amount of the rent!"`

"Twenty rix-dollars current money per year, but twelve per half-year, sir. Kindly —"

Cold, gloomy, cutting words! "But I should be ashamed not to go up, when I have come here," he reflected. He flew up the stairs.

The woman conducted him into two small rooms with roses on the wall-paper. "Please sit down and examine them, at any rate," said she, went out, and shut the door.

"Sit down? No, indeed! Great God, what business have I here? But what splendid rooms! pleasant, divinely pleasant! They have been scrubbed very recently, almost as if it had been done last night; they have been put in order, swept, and have had fresh curtains put up. It is clear that a guest was expected. And gillyflowers in the windows! Look, what mirrors and frames! The frames of glass too, with gilt paper underneath. That was it exactly. And the inner room? Rosy wall-paper there also, but a little different. Oh, if I could only live here, and—if—that is to say, if—Good God! It is certain it was these rooms that she dreamed about that night in Arboga, when—"

The door opened. She stepped in. The sergeant was a little startled at the sight of a black-dressed girl, a girl in a serge dress, with Sara's head, who was mildly smiling at his amazement. She wore a broad, finely starched lawn collar over her breast; her cheeks were white.

"I am in mourning, as you see," she said.

"How glad I am! You alive? You smiling?" he exclaimed.

Her sorrow was painted like a delicate twilight around the uppermost parts of her eyes, but the enamel of the white reflected a bluish tinge as never before, and the pupils sparkled. "Albert!" she cried.

He did not answer; he just looked.

"How do you like these rooms? Do you want to rent them? But you cannot know them very well yet. May I not invite you down to my place, and then you can see how I am fixed? Breakfast is waiting. And if you don't start right off again on your trips, this very day, I'll invite you down to dinner also. Will all this do, Albert?"

Still he said nothing. But in the whole expression of his face was the answer: "It will do."

Epilogue[1]

IT is said that a light veil hangs suspended before the future of Europe and prevents us from observing clearly the forms that beckon to us from within. I believe it. The veil is not entirely transparent; in several places its beautiful drapery hangs down in somewhat thicker folds than in others, and there it is the less penetrable to our sight. It would be ignoble if we should entertain a feeling of curiosity in regard to such elevated matters and presumptuous if we should pretend to describe with certainty what is happening behind the veil in a time yet unborn, which God has in part purposely obscured. But it is imperative, nevertheless, and worthy of man, to divine as much of the path that we and our children must follow as is necessary to take the right direction. Nobody can or may know his particular line of action in the future; but the general—the real—line of direction is clearly indicated, because the mysterious veil is only in part a jealous and impenetrable fabric; it reveals the way, but conceals the details of it. These, however, can be discerned more and more as we hurry onward.

After all, man must sometime learn to know himself; it cannot be prevented. The more candidly, the better; I cannot believe otherwise. What has been the result of thousand-year-old falsehoods?

[1] This Epilogue appears as an Introduction in the original.

Society built on them totters to its very foundations. What kind of fruit has the individual har-
vested from the perpetual hypocrisy to which he
has been forced? Forced, I say. Simply this: that
the fruit has become real immorality with the title
of morality; and another fruit has followed as a by-
product—real unhappiness with the title of happiness.

It is clear that here we must concern ourselves
with those *problems of the times*, or one of them, that
have come to be so general. They can be post-
poned, but not avoided. They belong to a category
of subjects that all think about and no one dares
mention, a category of very poor repute. If, and
whenever, it enters into a discourse, it is badly explained, misrepresented, and condemned, because
it contains one of the germs for the salvation of
humanity in moral relations. History can furnish
only a small number of examples where the teach-
ers of mankind, taken as a whole, have not avoided
the helpful, detested means of rescue, misnamed
deliverance itself as destruction, and as an aid against
it have conjured up all evil at their command and
sanctified it by calling it good. When the work of
an age tends unceasingly to save, help, and improve
the soul, they cry just as unceasingly that the times
are materialistic: they fail to see that their own institutions, established for morality, lead to real vices,
or at least do not prevent them. This is manifestly

a fact, whatever their intentions may be. We calum-
niate nobody; we pronounce a benediction on all.

' With regard to the problems that confront the
age to come, weep if you will, you cannot retard
them. The gradually approaching salvation of humanity and morals cannot be avoided.

You may *say*, to be sure, that human beings now-
adays deteriorate through "material interests" and
become more and more physical; you can assert
that so long as you do not realize that it is the soul
which our age is really working for above all. It
is the rescue of the beautiful and innocent at the
bottom of our spirit; it is the reanimation of the
truly good, of the idealistically hopeful, which God
has permitted because He has created it. It is a
question really of the defense of the only thing in
life that has value, or ought to have value, to man;
and of a heaven that has been misjudged for thousands of years. The interest in this is called earthly;
is there any meaning to the expression? It is the
desire to possess a glimpse of heaven on earth, a
glimpse which God must have intended us to desire, since He created it Himself. But men have
chased this glimpse of heaven away, and are still
chasing it away as much as they can, because they
consider it fully necessary to make themselves miserable in big things, not in little. On the contrary,
almost all institutions are intended to aid in the
little affairs of life, to insure the ownership of the

insignificant, and to make us happy in trifles, so long as they succeed in making our happiness in the big and real world an absolute impossibility. This strange endeavor has for its first cause a motive worthy of a certain respect, but its consequences threaten to disorganize humanity and to banish, together with happiness, all morality. Now what can be so estimable in its intentions, but so disastrous in its consequences? Why, through a misjudgment of what good habits and happiness are *per se*, that is, according to the true nature of man, one has come to believe that deep piety can be attained only through a simultaneous destruction of personality; in other words, only by a person in whom all individual characteristics are crushed or made void. Men have believed the moral to be merely the general, which has, therefore, been called the pure. Neither have they realized that, in the privacy of all personality, only that is repudiable which is contrary to the true purpose of creation in any particular person; while any other individual trait in him, far from being subject to expulsion, is in itself the one condition through which he may become what he should. And so, with all our honorable intentions, we are confronted with the result that good morals do not spring up on earth from annihilation and violation of what is individual. Even through hells of torture, no true virtue is attained. Is then the attainment of pure virtue a

treasure inaccessible to man? It is our opinion that
the mystery of morality must be solved simultane-
ously with the mystery of happiness. It is man's
highest problem to find harmony between true,
pure morality and true, pure happiness of the larger,
comprehensive kind. If at any period or in any
particular instance both may not be united, and
one must be put aside temporarily, then we may
sacrifice happiness, since in that case virtue is more
important: for this conviction we are willing to die
and become martyrs. The one great purpose of society must be to produce harmony between the two:
everything else is false or small. To suffer what is
unnecessary for the right is a wrong martyrdom, cow-
ardly to men and condemnable before God. Christian society may no longer cling to heathen ideas
about revenge and external sacrifice, which funda-
mentally amount to nothing, and to which Christ
has put an end: if we but follow Him!

What we have noted up to this time should be
further expounded. We neither can nor desire to
see theses on these subjects. We are mistaken if
we think that scientific systems of any value may
be devised in all fields beforehand. We must first
learn to know people themselves, observe them in
their nooks and corners, listen to their innermost
sighs, nor scorn to understand their tears of joy.
In brief, what we need are true stories or sketches
from life: examples, contributions, and experiences.

We may make any reflections we please about these experiences; we may condemn them, or we may consider them dangerous. But if the experiences are genuine, they constitute, no matter how peculiar, the essential preliminaries, the indispensable conditions for a correct knowledge of the matter. For only then have we anything to discuss; only then can we state what is to be disapproved, and, again, what should be approved. Upon such foundations, built from the inner experiences of man, philosophy may appear to construct along all of its various lines a complete system, to develop, to teach, to give counsel. Some one may assert, by way of objection, that philosophers and law-makers have always followed this order; that, however, is historically false. Only a very few, and most of those from ancient times, have gathered their knowledge of man from life itself as a source, and then written about it. Thousands of later philosophers, through chamber-study and mere reading of what others have written, have arrived at conclusions and formulated systems which are noteworthy for the understanding of their own biographies and hermetical trends of thought, yet are a real scourge and a spiritual corruption to humanity when they have succeeded in becoming an active force in the commonwealth. We shall deeply respect philosophy; we shall prostrate ourselves before it, when it is once born.

The manuscript that I unfold here contains the narrative of an episode only. In this episode not everything possible has happened, of course, that may belong to the subject; consequently it alone cannot serve as a foundation for any thesis, which should always fulfill the requirements of a complete conception of its prescribed goal. Still it would please me if this episode should be considered not too trivial by the reader and the characters in it not too insignificant. What they tell each other and what they do means actually, in the first place, nothing more than that they tell it to each other and act as they do; just in this particular the narrative constitutes an experience, a fact, a sketch from life. To condemn or approve this fact belongs to the thesis. Consequently, to determine whether their sayings or doings may be applied to others depends upon something else besides the narrative. We meet here the *noli me tangere* of our age. The flower of our century is a sensitive Mimosa, whose easily irritable nerve-fibres shudder and shrink together hastily around the crown at every hand that is bold, cold, and rude enough to attempt with the very fingers to get at such chaste leaves. She loves to be understood, but not to be touched.

THE CHAPEL

[Kapellet]

1838

THE CHAPEL

A Day

> "It is a profound truth that old age in every century looks upon youth as its high priest, its leader, help, and strength. The world depends upon young elements for its progress. God Himself was only thirty-three when He died for humanity and introduced, through the cross, a new ideal of life."

A YOUNG man of twenty-three with a very pleasant face and an open, happy countenance had just climbed into a poor, shabby-looking cart and sat down. He turned around and found his little bulging carpet-bag tightly closed and securely tucked away back of the seat. So he took the reins, let the horse start off at a slow trot, and drove out of the city of Kalmar through the south gate. He nodded his farewell to the high, broad, turf-covered walls, crossed the bridge over the deep moat that encircles the town, passed through the so-called Old City, which is now only a suburb of its daughter, the new Kalmar, and after a while reached the wide road to Vassmolösa.

As soon as the traveler found himself in the middle of the main highway, he gave the reins to the postboy who sat at his left, and amused himself with reflections. He had just been ordained in the magnificent cathedral of the Kalmar bishopric, an edifice that has few equals in Sweden for architectural beauty. With deep, devotional joy, he reviewed in his mind the whole sublime ceremony through which he had been consecrated a servant of God and a special friend of mankind. He had felt no little gratification when he had immediately received an appointment as assistant pastor in one of the most beautiful parishes in Södra Möre, among the islands along the coast near Blekinge. He was now on his way there. It was early Sunday morning, and he was to preach his first sermon to-day in his future parish. The church was not very far from Kalmar, so that he could easily drive the whole distance before the service.

The reader may think that a curate on his way to the pastor in charge ought to have started a few days earlier than the time set for his official appearance before a congregation, but duties that cannot be mentioned here had kept him in Kalmar at the home of the old widow of Bishop Stagnelius, and since he already knew personally his prospective superior, Rector X in Y, and had also corresponded with him concerning the date of his arrival, he saw nothing offensive in this tardiness.

It was half-past five in the morning; the birds were singing, and the sun was smiling most delightfully on the traveler. He passed by Ljungby, but it was altogether too early to go and pay his respects to the bishop, even if he had had the desire or opportunity; and so he drove on, reached Vassmolösa soon afterward, and changed horses.

The country district of Möre became more and

more pleasing the farther south he went. He had already arrived at Värnaby. Here he stepped down while the fresh horse was being hitched to the cart, and decided to take a walk through the park over to the Värnanäs manor house, which was situated nearby. He told his postboy to drive along the highway alone and wait on the other side of the estate near the familiar big, black gate.

As soon as one enters Värnaby, one distinguishes to the south four tall poplars that stand very near the Värnanäs manor and serve as a landmark far and wide, without disclosing the house itself until one arrives in the immediate neighborhood. Few places in Sweden possess such charm as the park through which the young curate was now passing. The picture does not owe its charm to melancholy and picturesque poverty. No, indeed. Richness and fertility surround the wanderer here; he is treading the soil of Oxenstjerna. The youth strolled along the winding path through a field with grass as tall as himself, and admired the numerous oaks with dark green, luxuriant crowns that were visible everywhere above the meadow. God's kindness, manifested toward man even on earth, was revealed here in all its fullness and abundance. The consecrated young man walked with religious care lest he injure even the merest blade of grass, and his heart filled with silent prayer. He did not remember now the words of his written sermon, which he carried in his breast pocket, but he felt disposed to speak holy words to the people without any preparation whatever, except twenty-three years spent in piety and virtue with poor, loving parents.

When he had crossed the meadow, he came to the broad private road of red gravel that runs between Värnanäs and the sea. He followed it until he reached the old wooden house near the shore, in which the counts of Södra Möre had themselves perhaps lived, and which now, because of its architecture, presented a strange appearance in contrast with buildings of our own time. After the young curate had hastily inspected this memorial of olden days, he walked back again on the red road and entered the new garden of Värnanäs. Up to this time he had not met a living soul! Silently he followed the circuitous gravel walks, crossed the small bridges over the canals, and finally began to wonder how he should find the shortest path to the main highway, where his cart was waiting. At this moment of perplexity, a nurse girl of about eleven or twelve years came along. She was pulling a little carriage filled with various round bundles looking like children's garments. It was evident that under ordinary circumstances the owner of the swaddling-clothes rode in this little vehicle and that the nurse girl, presumably, was accustomed to do the pulling; but now there were only linen things in it, and it occurred to the curate that the pretty little servant girl was taking them so early in the morning to rinse them in the stream and then return with them to her little master, who would probably wake up about breakfast time.

What trifling thoughts for a minister! But the girl with her serious, slightly pale, and extremely interesting face, such as children sometimes have, was the only person whom he saw in this whole beautiful landscape. Of her he inquired the way. Thereupon she walked ahead of him, with her little cart, along several winding gravel walks, through the magnificent park. He noticed that in order to direct him she took a path that led her far away from the canals of the garden, her real destination. At last they reached the manor house itself. There it stood in all its glory, painted yellow and newly repaired, sheltered by the four towering poplars he had seen from afar! The road to the gate opening on the main thoroughfare passed close by the place, and he asked the girl not to trouble herself any further. At the parting he patted her kindly on the head; she had beautified the attractive morning landscape with childlike charm, and her little curtsy at his farewell was full of expression. At the very moment that he was thus gently patting and stroking her hair, he happened to cast his eyes up toward a window of the manor house. A curtain was just being raised, and he met the glance of an elderly woman in a neat nightcap standing beside the rising curtain.

The young man, however, was not disturbed by this. He knew that the wife of Major Manner-skantz, the owner of Värnanäs, was now at home, and had her two daughters-in-law with her; but time did not permit him to pay them his respects. Therefore he went directly to the black gate near the broad Kalmar road; the cart was already there, and he climbed in and drove away.

For a time he continued on toward Påboda, but soon he turned off the highway, beyond a beautiful, poetic place called Segelmara, and followed the narrow course that was to take him to his superior. He had not reached the rocky coast itself. His heart beat more violently the nearer he came to the beloved temple where he was presently to appear. The path was becoming narrower and narrower and more overgrown; he was approaching a bay of the sea. Soon he had only a short distance to go to the parsonage and the mother church. Just then, however, at an almost hidden bypath, he met a man who made a very polite bow and asked our traveler if he was the assistant pastor. Receiving an affirmative answer, the man, a kind of parish runner, delivered a message from the rector. It directed his new colleague not to drive up to the church, but to proceed westward to the skerries and give his sermon there in the chapel, for word had come that the chaplain in that place had suddenly fallen ill.

"Since the time is short—" continued the messenger, with a bow—

"I will go there at once," interrupted the good-natured young man; "just make my apologies to the rector for not first paying him a visit in the rectory. I will start directly for the chapel."

"I will do so," answered the messenger, raising his hat.

Fortunately the postboy succeeded in finding the laborious serpentine path to the chapel. This path, however, extended only a part of the way over dry land. After a short time it came to an end at the edge of the water. Here a ferryman came out of a hut and led the curate to his boat. Soon he was floating on the bay and saw before him on the opposite side the beautiful shore of a projecting headland.

After a few minutes' journey, when they had encircled the cape, the chapel came into view, white and inviting in the midst of the green landscape. What a picture! The mere fact that a church stood there—whether of stone or wood—was sufficient to make a profound impression. Here was a building erected only for love and peace! It was built for no worldly end, but for the immeasurable benefit of the spiritual life. Itself protected by an invisible guardian, it watched over the welfare of mankind. We see very few houses on earth whose walls we can look on without a certain feeling of horror, of greater or less repulsion, at the thought of the ugly things that may have been committed within them. But a church—what a wonderful house! Innocence seems to be its roof, divine care its walls, and reverence the stones of the pavement upon which mortals may tread securely and be safe from the turmoil of the world.

Even if the young clergyman who was being rowed to the chapel shared the public opinion of his day concerning the unpriestly character of various members of his profession, he had, nevertheless, already learned from the writings of open-hearted theologians the difference between religion and sophistry. Godliness is as good to-day as it was yesterday and will be to-morrow. Religion lives and rescues its beloved among mankind and in nature, although it may be concealed and obscured. Nothing stands in closer relation to nature, conceived in a pure and innocent sense, than religion, provided it is interpreted by man in the same spirit in which it is given.

The boat lay to, and the young man stepped ashore, reverently timid, as if walking on consecrated ground. The chapel was situated only a few stonethrows from the landing, but before he went up to it his eye was attracted by a gloomy, wretched hut near the water's edge from which six, seven, or eight ragged children emerged and stared curiously at the approaching stranger.

"This is Sunday," he thought, "and yet so poorly dressed. But—perhaps they have nothing better," he added in his mind.

He knew that the rocky coast region was often very poor, and wherever he looked the soil seemed very thin and stony, though a little verdure on the surface gave the landscape a smiling appearance, especially when seen from a distance. He walked up to the eight children. The youngest appeared to be a year old, and the others, two, three, four, and so on, chronologically in line, up to nine or ten years. Despite their rags, they were clean, and their faces were disfigured, not by dirt but by hunger. A certain expression of the eye, a marked similarity of look in all the youngsters, showed that they were brothers and sisters. The curate looked around in vain for the parents.

"Where is your father, my dear children; or," he added with a sudden inner fear, "where, at least, is your mother?"

The oldest of the group, a long-haired boy, answered, "Father is out to sea, and mother's gone to church, because it's Sunday to-day, sir."

"It is Sunday. Yes, children! Aren't you going to church, too?"

"No!" answered the one who so bravely had acted as spokesman, and his brothers and sisters showed by gestures and expression that they agreed with what he said.

"You're not? And why not?"

"Mother doesn't want the church people to see us, because, you see, we—on week days all the neighbors go dressed this way—but on Sundays they don't—"

"My dear children, you don't have to feel ashamed of your clothes before God; just come along to church. If you don't go to church, how will you get a chance to hear the word of God?"

"Oh, we'll get a chance, all right," he answered; "mother repeats the whole sermon to us when she comes home."

"Has your father been out to sea very long?"

"He went fishing several days ago. I think he'll be home late this afternoon with the rest of the fishermen from here."

"Do you fish on Sundays?"

"Of course we do."

"Then there is nobody in the chapel, I presume, to attend the service to-day, is there? The church hill is pretty well deserted."

"Oh, I guess, sir, everybody around here is in the chapel—old men, old women, and all the children who can go to church."

"Nobody but old men, old women, and children?"

"Oh, yes—and my mother, too—she's young, she—but the rest up there in the church are all old women, because, you see, all the people are off fish-

ing. Mother was the only one of the young folks
who didn't go with them, because she is sick at best,
and then she had to look after little Kersti and give
her something to eat, you see."

The curate ventured a glance into the hut, for
he had never been on the rocky island before. It
looked as if there had been nothing to eat in the
house for several days; at least the fire-place showed
no trace of anything which, though it might pos-
sibly be mixed with cinders, would nevertheless be
edible. Not the tiniest scrap of potato was to be
seen; nor was there any cupboard or cubby-hole
that might conceal the most indispensable articles
of food.

"Is everybody who belongs to the congregation
of this chapel as poor as that?"

"Poor! What do you mean, sir?"

The gentleman was a little amazed at the discov-
ery that this boy himself did not know what poverty
meant. "Why, my dear boy," he said, "I am asking if everybody who lives here is obliged to eat as
little as you, poor children."

"To eat as little as we?"

"Yes."

"Oh, we'll have plenty to eat, all right, just as
soon as father comes home with the fish. Yes, he
has stayed away for a long time—longer than the
others," added the boy with a glance to one side,
which in part concealed his sorrowful mood.

"How does it happen that you fish on Sunday?" questioned the pastor.

"Well, you see, sir, the fish don't keep any Sabbath, and therefore if we want any fish we can't keep it either, but have to go out with all kinds of tackle as soon as the schools come round, if we want to catch them."

"You may be right. Did you say your father had been away longer than the rest of the fishermen?"

"Yes, ever since the beginning of the week, sir, and that's a long time. Mother thinks he's crossed over to Öland, for Sven Carlson saw him lose his boat in the storm last Tuesday and just barely get away in another boat; but I think he'll come to-night with the big fishing party."

"And then you'll get food?"

"And then we can dance, sir, and that's better yet!"

The stranger was astonished at the cheerfulness of this youngster, for whom it meant less to satisfy several days' hunger than to have the pleasure of a dance. He liked the boy. He did not understand how it was, but he thought he had seen the same or a similar face somewhere before.

"See here," he remarked, "if you expect to dance and are not afraid of looking ragged before people, come along to church and don't be afraid of God any more."

"Oh, I tell you, sir, we can dance well enough.

When we 've got the fish on land, we are all as rich as the Lord himself; nobody cares how we look, and we sing — Heigh, ho! and Gee-ho! But to church, sir; no, thank you! I 'll never go there till father comes home from Ottenby, and mother thinks he 'll bring home some wadmal cloth for us all."

"Is n't she afraid that he has suffered distress at sea?"

"Oh, father can swim, he can, and if he has reached Öland, as Sven Carlson thinks, he has probably collected a bill for fish sold last spring to the Alum Works, and then he has bought wadmal and will be home with the big fishing party that 's expected to-night."

It was obviously impossible to make this young islander downhearted by any sad reflections; and the curate himself probably made them for the sole purpose of being able to comfort the children later, after the sorrow, with the aid of religion. But children do not come within the pale of religion, and very seldom need to be comforted, because they are not without comfort in the first place. They may whine and cry about little things, but the big problems of life are a merry game to them. After these observations the good curate went up to the church.

"I wonder what kind of a congregation I shall have to-day," he meditated.

Decrepit old men and women are also people. He stepped nearer. A man with a long and ugly face, walking on crutches, met him at the entrance, took off his cap, and exerted himself with a visible and arduous effort to raise the latch for "His Reverence"—as he muttered between his toothless jaws —and open the massive church door. The clergyman greeted him with a friendly bow and walked in. Gloomy indeed! From a distance on the sea this old chapel building had looked very pleasant and inviting surrounded by green meadows; but now it exposed to the eye of the visitor only dark slanting walls and old unpainted posts worn smooth with age, which supported in helter-skelter fashion either the roof itself or small projecting structures just beneath which did duty for galleries. The stranger had never before been in the outskirts of the parish and had never seen the chapel. He was acquainted only with the magnificent mother church, and knew only the more wealthy members and their environment; such was the picture he had had before his mind during the whole journey. Now, on the other hand, it was just as though he had entered into a new, unexpected, and very serious world. The dilapidated pews were dark brown from wear and not from paint, and there was no symmetry in their arrangement. It was clear that they had been built without strict use of square or level. As he walked slowly down the church aisle to the vestry, the young man looked around to get an idea of his prospective congregation. The pews were only partly filled; and yet there were thirty or forty people in scattered, thoughtful groups. At his approach they all rose to their feet gradually — that is to say, those who were able to get up; for although several lame and paralyzed members made a sideward and painful motion to rise from their seats and take part in the general silent greeting and expression of reverence for the pastor, they succeeded for the most part only with considerable discomfort and even agony. Was there not a single young person present? Not even the mother of those children? He looked around in vain for her. He was deeply moved and yet terrified at the sight of all the surrounding forms: some had extremely long chins; some were pale, bald-headed or almost bald except for tufts of hair scattered here and there; others were red-eyed or half blind; some noses were very pointed, while others turned up; everybody was hunchbacked; and both men and women had large, clumsy hands, presumably the result of their occupation. Wherever the young man turned, he heard slight rattlings in the pews, perhaps from a cane or from some bony knee that trembled against the pew door or could not remain quiet beside its own mate. There was little difference between the faces of the men and the women: the former no longer looked masculine; the latter were not particularly feminine. They resembled the insignificant result in a long example in subtraction, where the remain-

der had become very small, because the subtrahend
had been almost as large as the minuend; that is
to say, misery had so nearly consumed the vitality
and pleasing qualities of these mortals that their
residuum of life seemed almost nil. Seeing so many
scraggy and almost ghost-like figures, a cold perspiration appeared on the young man's brow, when
he remembered the sermon he had written and was
to give here. What is more common or natural for
young and newly ordained ministers, when they
write their first sermon, and especially when they
intend to make their initial appearance during the
summer time in large and popular churches of rich
and beautiful districts, before a congregation which,
to be sure, is composed half of peasants, but also
largely of a better class—what is more natural than
to adorn their prospective address with a flowery
language full of life and joy and overflowing with
beautiful pictures and pleasant comparisons? The
heart swells; the very finger that directs the pen
of the young homilist is poetical. Everything becomes enchanting; the gospel takes on the form of
an idyl, and the law becomes a gentle admonition.
All things are made to resemble the sun, the stars,
the hours of the day, the spring and the lilies and
even the winsome, gentle eye of the maiden. But
now! Before what or whom should this glowing
composition be read? In justice to the curate, let it
be said that his feeling of distress was not resent-

ment at seeing his beautiful work done for nought;
he was not vain, especially in such matters; but
he began, and rightly, to wonder how this address
would sound to this congregation, and what fruits
it would bear. Was he not the pastor for to-day of
these decrepit, half-crippled individuals? And did
they not have the right to hear the word of God
from him? What he had written when he sat in his
study had been intended for the young, lively members of the main church who were more in harmony
with himself; and perhaps there may have been
some one in particular for whom — who knows? —
for much enters unknowingly into the thoughts of
a writer. Was not this and that elegant expression
meant for some particular beautiful listener of the
fairer sex, I wonder? Is that so impossible — so pre-
posterous — or so odious? Not at all; it is very
human and very common. But now! What would
all that mean to his present auditors, whom he loved
also, whose pastor he was to-day, and to whom he
wished to speak words of comfort?

Disturbed by such perplexing thoughts, he
reached the end of the aisle and entered the small,
low vestry. There he was received by the cantor,
a nonagenarian patriarch with white, slightly curly
hair, so tall that, although he stooped as he came
forward to meet the entering curate, he was still
head and shoulders above him. "I understand that
the regular pastor of the chapel has fallen ill, and

therefore I have been commissioned by the rector to take the service here," reported the stranger.

"Quite right; yes, I know; you are welcome, Your Reverence, come in!" answered the cantor.

The curate, who had just been called "Your Reverence," crept far into the vestry and sought to muster up his courage. "God will provide the lamb for the offering," he said in an undertone to himself, while the cantor obligingly and without being requested assisted him with the gown, a relic of camlet material which always hung on a nail in the vestry for use on Sundays. A small fragment of mirror stood leaning against the grating of the window. The curate looked into it to see if his bands were straight. The mirror could only reflect the two strips besides the nethermost point of the chin; no further inspection was necessary at this toilet.

"How about the numbers of the hymns, sir?" questioned the gray-haired man behind him.

"Where is the organist?" inquired the minister. "I'll give the numbers to him."

"We don't keep any organist in the chapel," replied the cantor. "That would be a needless expense when there's no organ here. You can give me the numbers, for I do the singing before you enter the chancel."

No organ! So even this comfort would be denied the musical young pastor, who had so often been lost in divine blessedness during the mystical, solemn, and languishing harmonies of the hymns.

The aged comrade now took something out of one of the corner cupboards of the vestry and came up with a hymn-book as big as a Bible. Knips! Knips! sounded twice as he unclasped the enormous brass hooks that held the thick, black covers together.

"Here, Your Reverence, choose, if you have not made a list of the hymns." The letters of the opened book were as large uncials, and the type before him was so clear, bold, and coal black that if the curate had placed the volume at his feet he could still have read every word.

To try to find one of his favorite hymns in the book, Number 224 by Wallin or Number 2 by Franzén, proved futile. He had not the so-called "old hymn-book" before him, but the old, old one, a contemporary of Jesper Svedberg, which had been revised during the reign of Charles XI.

"Do the people use this hymn-book?" asked the pastor.

"No, sir, I use it, and the people sing after me," answered the cantor; "nobody here uses a book except myself."

A grim, austere seriousness, both Carolinian and Lutheran, began to seize the newly arrived minister as if with claws, but he was a man of the spirit, and therefore felt a spiritual inspiration. He turned over a few pages and examined a verse here and there. "Take this hymn," he said, "then sing this one as I enter the pulpit, and later this one here—and finally this for the concluding hymn."

"Very good, sir, I couldn't have chosen better myself." The cantor left the vestry.

With long but firm steps, the patriarch went out into the church and hung up the selected numbers on the hymn-board. It was a solemn though now unnecessary custom, for no one present had a hymnal save himself. He struck up a tune, took his position in front near the altar where the cantor's black pew was located, and in a loud tone began his singing. His voice was harsh and sometimes shrill, but it did not tremble, and no quavers were audible. He had hardly finished the first introductory line when everybody joined in the hymn, and the officiating pastor appeared in the door of the vestry to listen and take part.

What voices! Those skeleton forms could sing, every one!

As he stood there, the curate felt his heart throb with emotion. Among the thirty or forty singers there was not a single beautiful voice, but they kept in tune in both the upper and lower register. They sang in strict unison, accompanying each other with rigid exactness, as is the custom in congregations without an organ. Moreover, all was so disciplined and correct that it seemed as if a corporal were giving a singing lesson. There he stood right in front of them. It was evident that he would tolerate no nonsense. At every cadence, he drew his bushy eyebrows high up on his forehead and looked down with joy and happiness upon his children, these old men and women who had presumably been at one time his pupils. The unisonant song grew so strong sometimes that it seemed to lift the roof, and some of the windows rattled noisily. Now and then the curate looked at the mighty cantor. A little while before he had felt like a son of the congregation; now he felt like a grandchild of the hoary master who was singing in the choir.

"And I am to preach to these people!" said he to himself.

The hymn was finished, and the pastor went before the altar to begin the service. He found the prayer-book there already opened for him. After reading the introductory prayer, he turned toward the congregation with the book in his hand. His voice, a little unsteady at first, became strong, full, and beautiful, as he read the prescribed holy words.

While reading he looked up now and then at those in the pews before him, for whose benefit he was reading. What did he see? Were these the same people?

There were the same bony, pale faces, but with glistening eyes and heads stretched forward in wrapt attention. "What has not the hymn accomplished already! The spirit of the Lord is with us!" thought

the man at the altar. His courage increased; his
voice grew constantly steadier, louder, and more
powerful, as he went on reading from the service-
book.

"I poor, miserable sinner, both conceived and
born in sin, and likewise through all of my days—"
He had never read those words as he did to-day;
he sank down upon the cushion before the altar,
glowing with a new feeling. Frail sinners were kneel-
ing everywhere before him. It became light about
him in the low, gloomy temple; his own ears listened with astonishment to the words spoken by his
own mouth: devotion flowed in lofty rhythms from
his lips. Now, as he knelt, he himself learned what
he taught the others.

After the Confession of Sins he arose, and, with
a creaking sound, the whole congregation rose too.
The wretched were borne on the wings of grace,
and the weak were given strength to stand. Before
the preacher turned around again, he looked at
them with burning, hasty glances. "And I—a sinner—I am to preach to these people!" he meditated. "How shall I do it! And yet, see how all
their eyes are turned toward me! They are hungry
for words of comfort! Oh, my God! What—what
shall I say to them?" With this overwhelming self-
consciousness he turned toward the altar in the
usual manner and read the remaining prescribed
prayers from his book.

He passed out of the chancel. The whole congregation followed the movements of the stranger with eagerly strained eyes. It was no longer from curiosity alone, for apparently they felt that he had read to them from the bottom of his heart. He went back to the vestry, and another hymn, "the pulpit verse," was sung.

While the cantor was singing, the newly ordained, inexperienced clergyman fell on his knees alone in the vestry. No honest man ever felt himself in a greater or more perturbing embarrassment. He turned white as a sheet when he heard the last strains of the pulpit verse. Now it was finished! He had to go — he *had* to — and he had to *preach!*

With a great effort he mastered his feelings, went out into the church, and mounted the pulpit.

No congregation ever received its minister more quietly, without the slightest sound. It was not only because he was so young and new to them; but a wonderful atmosphere of spiritual humility — of exalted shame — surrounded him with its radiance. There seemed to be a halo of modesty around him, not of awkwardness, but, to repeat, of shame. It is a mysterious fear that a young man feels when he suddenly finds himself face to face with heaven and earth as the spokesman of God.

For a while he did not say a word. His pale face, his shining eyes, and the long silence all contributed to increase the attention of the old people.

Every one who could see looked at him and at him
alone. He noticed this, and it made his nerves still
more tense. Finally, with his eyes turned toward
heaven, he opened his lips: "Father, I have sinned;
before Thee I have done evil!" he uttered with
a weak but melodious and therefore very audible
voice.

Was this his text? It would have been most natural to see him put his hand in his pocket, pull out
his notes, and preach from them. But — he had
folded his hands and could not unclasp them. He
did not recall a word of his written sermon; he did
not even remember that it existed.

After these words he was again silent and looked
around. The congregation waited in vain for him
to give the chapter and verse of the text, according to the usual custom. The words were inscribed
in his heart, but he did not state that.

"Father, I have sinned! I have transgressed
against Thee and against my fellow men!" Again
he was silent.

It is a profound truth that old age in every century looks upon youth as its high priest, its leader,
help, and strength. The world depends upon young
elements for its progress. God Himself was only
thirty-three when He died for humanity and introduced, through the cross, a new ideal of life.

Every hero, every leader, every founder has been
a young man. Afterward come senates of vener-

able men who undertake to formulate and carry out his ideas. And they guard his enterprises, until a new youth appears who leads them forward another step, whereupon old legislators again begin to execute, maintain, and preserve. This is the character of true progress. Only one young man was God, but He led the way for all the rest. Every upright, well-informed, venerable old man knows this is true; it always has been, and must be in the future if all shall go well.

But when old people are gathered around their young leader — as in this chapel — with their eyes full of confidence, waiting to hear his voice admonishing them and pointing out the right path, it is sublime to see him stand there silent! Silent, for he is ashamed, and casts his eyes confidently toward heaven.

It is noble for a young man to be honest. Then he is not a charlatan. The curate was speechless, for what could he say? Still he hopefully directed his glances upward.

For the third time he opened his lips and said: "Father, forgive me! Forgive me for what I have ventured — I have dared to appear among these people as your prophet! I who would speak to you am a sinner; and you who expect words of comfort and grace from me are sinners. What shall we say to each other? Let us pray. Almighty God, our Lord, King of Heaven and Earth, Lord of Hosts, God of Sabaoth. Consider not our wretchedness. Our infirmity lies before Thee; our bones are crushed, and the Angel of Death breathes upon our withered limbs. But thou, O Lord, dost not trample upon the fallen; Thou dost not quench the smoking flax; and Thou sendest food from Thy table to him who eateth among dogs. We come to Thee hungry and naked; our souls are in the dark, and our bodies are in the cold. Christ Jesus, Thou Sun of Grace, rise and spread Thy light over the land of the unrighteous: the ground is parched, and its wide fissures yawn from thirst. Our basins contain no water, the clouds are sealed and give no rain. But we have learned that Thou lovest us! Thou hast not despised the wretched! O Lord, how couldst Thou care for us? Thou hast descended and shown mercy to the blind. Thou hast healed the leper and raised the dead. Thou hast not scorned to eat with sinners: Thou art our friend! Thou hast interceded for us with Thy Father: Thou hast sweat blood from deep anguish. Thou hast delivered Thyself into the hands of the enemy for our sake, and hast not feared the cross. Thou, O Son, Jesus Christ, who hath conquered death, art my choice this day, and my heart loves Thee. I know that I may share the fruits of Thy victory, and I believe that Thou wouldst call me Thine. Thou art my Health. All the clouds of sin have disappeared. I love Thee, O Lord, above all things, above all things in heaven and earth. Thou art the One who renewest all for me. My limbs were crushed, but now they have been made whole. I believe that Thou wilt love me! Pains will then pass away, and my dying soul will be revived. The vesture of my spirit was black, but I will cast off my wicked character and flee from my evil ways. Yet what am I able to do? Thou alone hast strength; let Thy blood flow into my veins, that I may become a new person, such as I have never been before."

Thus he continued, and his whole introduction became one unbroken prayer. Finally he bowed his head to repeat the Lord's prayer silently with the congregation. As he stood leaning against the pulpit and was about to say Amen, he happened to cast his eyes toward a corner of the church that he had not observed before. There he discovered a figure which did not seem old. "That is surely *their* mother, and she has probably lost her husband at sea," he thought. Because of her rags, it seemed, she had hidden herself in this corner. She looked consumptive and exhausted from overwork. In her emaciated face her eyes seemed very large and glistened with a light that was half despair and half love.

The preacher, who up to this time had merely improvised his introduction, suddenly remembered that he ought to have a subject for his sermon. An unprepared speaker has the advantage of being susceptible to reciprocal impressions from his audience and can thereby enter into an even more intimate relation or union with them. When the address is written in a study it is certain to answer the purpose at home; but whether it will pass over the heads of the prospective listeners is something one cannot know. The preacher got up and read the Gospel for the day: it was the fifth Sunday after Trinity and told of the miraculous draught of fishes, Luke v. After he had read it, he said: "The subject for our consideration this morning will be 'God feeds the fatherless at His table and lends His ear to the prayer of the widow.'"

When he repeated this, the congregation rose, as was the custom, but the members looked at him with not a little astonishment, for they had not heard such a topic from the pulpit before, even though it resembled a Scriptural text. Every one present had lost a father, husband, or wife. Every word he spoke struck home. He linked his subject and text together, and told how Christ had called fisher-folk to be His first disciples and they had become fishers of men. But how should that be done henceforth? Not by going out among the heathen and preaching to them, as Peter had gone, but by doing godly acts of charity in mutual sympathy among themselves, loving, feeding, and clothing one another. In this way they would win one another, and would all be won for God. They would gather one another in and would themselves be gathered:

they were fishermen, but also fishes caught in God's great draught. "And how does God feed the fatherless at His table?" he continued. "God gives food and raiment to orphans even in this life, when people imbued with His spirit receive them into their homes; for charity practiced by man is God's own charity, and He lends His ear to the prayers of the broken-hearted when His spirit exhorts, calls, and compels the man of means to help him who has nothing."

Obviously, there was nothing remarkable in the clergyman's presentation, unless it be that he adapted his method to his congregation; and it seemed strange to be addressed as fishermen, which they had always been. He spoke with both fervor and sense; he simply talked as one friend to another, and finally felt so much at home in the pulpit that his sermon resembled an interesting conversation, which, naturally, is always carried on without notes. The curate said nothing wonderful, worthy of record; but the greatness of Christianity lies in being small, and the road to blessedness is like the narrow and hardly visible path through a green meadow, where oaks grow, and a few lofty poplars mark the distant goal.

When the minister saw how the congregation seemed cheered, his own spirits rose with Christian joy, and at last the leaning old chapel appeared to him a home of light. "This is the Father's forgiveness," he concluded, "that we believe in the Son; for when Christ gives us life by living within us so that we flee from sin, then sin has no more power, and wrath cannot harm us. This is like a candle put in a dark room: he who hath no faith is already condemned; but whosoever believeth in the Son and remaineth steadfast in love shall never be judged. Amen.''

The people passed out of the church. It was noon-time and a very beautiful summer day.

Outside the chapel the curate was greeted again by a few lame and tottering figures, who lingered there and by their kind glances seemed to express appreciation of the sermon. Afterwards, like the rest, they crawled into their respective homes.

"Where shall I go for dinner?" This trivial thought passed through his mind when he was walking alone near the church. He had been up since five o'clock, had driven many miles, and, prosaically speaking, was hungry.

He pictured in his mind the woman in the chapel corner. It was strange he did not see her outside. In all probability she had gone home to her children, who were perhaps hungrier than she, because they were in good health.

After a short time he reached the top of a hill, which offered a broad view, not only over the environs of the chapel, but far out to sea. Here he saw a silent, motionless figure resting against a high, sharp, moss-covered stone, her eyes constantly fixed on the water. He approached and found it was she. There stood the mother gazing into the distance after the father.

"How do you do?" he said.

The poor woman started. She recovered, however, when she recognized the man who had just preached so consolingly to her and promised her children a father. Her face was no longer attractive; yet he could plainly see that she was one of those in whom the physical form had once been beautiful while the soul was so still.

"Come, my friend, and let us go to your children," he said. "They are waiting for you; it is time for dinner."

"Pastor," she answered, "I am expecting the south fishing-fleet home. It ought to be here soon."

"Is your husband with the fleet?"

She looked at him astonished, as though asking if he knew her history. "Jonas," she replied slowly, "is a wild and daring sea-bird."

"Jonas? Is your husband's name—"

"God only knows where he is. But if he is n't drowned, he ought to come home with the fleet, sir."

"Have confidence! But you must n't stand there gazing on the gloomy sea; come along with me and we 'll go to your children."

"You, pastor, visit us? No—oh, no—"

"Don't be distressed, it is Sunday to-day; come!"

She turned away from the water and followed the good, friendly minister. After walking a short distance together they met the tall, gray-haired old cantor, who seemed to be looking for the curate and, as soon as he saw him, came forward almost with open arms. "Your Reverence," he said, "I have been looking for you; I have a modest question to ask, provided it will give no offense."

"Not at all, my friend."

"Well, you see — our regular chaplain, Mr. Ek, is ill. He lives in the parsonage three miles from this church; and if Your Reverence wants to visit him this noon — following the general custom of ministers — the only way, reverend sir, is to walk, for we fishermen don't keep horses — and — "

"I have no intention of visiting him; I don't know him."

"Ah, I'm glad of that. Well, I thought, pastor, if you wouldn't refuse a poor old cantor, why I have a simple — very simple dinner to offer, the kind that less fortunate and lower-class people have."

"This man must be educated," thought the curate, "since he has learned as a preamble to depreciate his own value and count himself among the lower classes, which is done only by so-called cultured people." This self-abasement made a bad impression on the young man. Nevertheless he answered very kindly: "I thank you for the invitation. I have never accustomed myself to rich food."

"Well, then—that's fine—please come along with me and enter my humble cottage." He pointed toward the buildings south of the church, and his house was obviously the highest and largest of them all. "Do come, pastor; but I must make a humble apology, for I am a widower, you see, and another has charge of the household, that is—Still, I hope Your Reverence will pardon all."

"Thank you, cantor, but I have already been invited to dinner."

"What?" said the patriarch, straightening up and looking around astonished. "Where? By whom? Is it possible that any one has got ahead of me? I don't believe there is any one in the chapel who can entertain you, pastor."

"I am to take dinner with this woman and her children."

Nobody can describe the expression in the face of the other two at this answer. The poor woman, pale, yet secretly glad, looked at the curate with strange alarm. The cantor wrinkled his nose.

"With her? Do you know this woman, worthy sir?"

"I have only just met her to-day."

"She has eight or nine children, Your Reverence —whether she has a chair to sit on, I cannot say; and as for anything to eat, it will certainly not be food — hm — but, of course, the gentry always like to have their joke."

"I am not joking. I am well aware that my good hostess is poor, for I have already been in her house and seen her children."

Sudden blushes and pallor alternated on the face of the astonished mother.

"But," continued the curate, "I am poor myself, and I am the servant of Him who has promised His kingdom to every pious sufferer."

"You don't know this woman, my dear sir. I'm ashamed to say she's the worst in the whole neighborhood. I don't mean she's the poorest, for who isn't poor and miserable, alas! on this coast of ours; nor yet the most stupid, although no sensible person would have so many children, and we in these barren skerries look out for that; but," he added hastily, when he saw the curate's indignation, "her father was — "

"Oh — keep still! You hold your tongue, Ola Svenson!" cried the woman.

A lofty, almost noble anger appeared suddenly on her countenance when she heard her father mentioned.

"Yes — Your Reverence," interrupted the cantor, "you should know with what kind of people you are associating and the places you visit, so that you won't soil your own hands, as they say. Because her father was a thief, sir, a big thief, who was flogged at the whipping-post in Kalmar. I know all about it —everybody knows it here —and the 'sins of the fathers shall be visited upon'—"

"Has she herself ever stolen anything?" asked the clergyman with a stern look at the patriarch.

"Oh—no, I don't say that. No, indeed, I'm sure she hasn't. She is honest, all right, so far as that goes, and if anybody should accuse her of dishonesty, I'd be the first to defend her, for I have known her ever since she was a child, and she used to sing for me; but her father was a thief, and that's the reason she's so poor."

"I'll tell you, father, how that Scripture verse reads which you began to quote but did not finish. God says, the sins of the fathers shall be visited upon the children 'of them that hate me,' and mercy shown 'unto thousands of them that love me'— Have n't you heard that? The glory and good deeds of the fathers, as you well know, will not bring honor to mean and worthless children; neither will the transgressions of the fathers bring evil and disgrace to children who are more worthy than their parents. It may be that she has to struggle with poverty as a consequence of her father's crime, to which you refer; and yet much of her suffering may be the fault of her neighbors, if they are unkind or foolish enough to refuse aid to defenceless individuals who have done no harm and are merely the victims of their parents' mistakes. But

God loathes such injustice and will help all sufferers not helped by man. I am still determined to be the guest of this mother and her children. Perhaps we shall have nothing for dinner — I have not had anything to eat since five this morning — and yet—"

The cantor turned away with a slight bow, angrily muttering between his teeth: "I should think they ought to find out what kind of people they are dealing with and make some distinction. But that's the way of those young cocks when they first come out of the seminary. When they get older, they'll change," he added quietly to himself, and walked off.

The other two left the chapel hill and finally came to the seashore, where the little hut was situated, secluded and apart from the village. The ragged children came running out, and soon the mother was so surrounded that she could hardly walk. The oldest boy, whom we know already as the spokesman of his brothers and sisters, opened the door with a bearing that lacked neither politeness nor charm.

A pleasant odor welcomed the party in the doorway. The mother's face brightened immediately. The children had decorated the room with boughs and leaves and strewn chopped spruce on the floor to please her when she returned from church. "Jonas will like this when he comes," she said, and walked in.

"Mother, you are rich," said the curate, "to have so many children, and all so healthy and active! It is unfortunate that you seem to be a little sickly now; perhaps that is due to overwork. But try to be happy, don't get weary; soon your husband will come home, and there will be lots of fish in the house."

"Fish! Fish! Fish!" This treble cry from all the children had both a fearful and a highly characteristic tone. They were islanders—"ichthyophagists" —to whom fish is the embodiment of all good things in life. Fish represents money, clothes, house, and home, because it is the means of obtaining all these. There was something very coarse in the exclamation, but it was softened in the curate's ear when he remembered that one must forgive starving children for calling out the name of their first, greatest, and most innocent necessity with a certain wild and feverish enthusiasm.

"Keep still, youngsters!" commanded the mother.

"Tell me," said the curate, to change this unpleasant subject, "have you ever been in Kalmar? I don't understand; but it seems to me I have seen your face somewhere."

"No," she answered, "I was born on one of these islands, and have never been in any city except Karlskrona," she added with a very melancholy but sweet expression in her face.

"That was to see grandpa, sir, in jail," uttered the nine-year-old spokesman cheerfully and, as it seemed, entirely ignorant of both the purpose of the prison and his grandfather's fate.

The young clergyman shuddered. "Let's not talk about it," he said, again changing the subject. "You have a good many children; I assume that you haven't lost any."

"No," she replied, "they are all living."

"This is God's method of bestowing His blessing. We seldom hear of very poor people losing any children."

"It's a great joy, too, when one has anything to give them, the poor things, and one need not be afraid they may be driven to become at last—"

What they might become she did not say audibly. But the simple, artless boy, the oldest son, exclaimed without mercy, "Thieves? Oh, no—we won't be like grandpa, no, sir! I'm going to be a sailor, and go far, far away like my father and earn lots of money and come home and get grandpa out of jail."

Such are the pictures painted by youth with all its hope and enthusiasm! Even the mother caught the boy's cheerful spirit, a sudden glimmer of joy passed over her emaciated face, and her big eyes began to glisten.

Again the curate tried to change the topic of the conversation by saying, "Haven't you the largest brood of children in the whole village? I dare say the cantor has n't very many."

"The cantor? He has no children, sir. He had one son who died several years ago; so it's no wonder he is rich and lays by large sums of money every year from fish, since he has nobody to eat it up."

"Still he does not have our Lord's greatest blessing. God loves him less than you, and he seemed to me rather proud and uncharitable."

"You must n't think ill of him, pastor; he is quite a nice old fellow and not wicked, though he is the richest and most prominent man in the skerries. He has five boats in the big fishing-fleet, sailed by his own crew, so you must expect him to be a little haughty. I used to sing pretty hymns for him when I was a little girl, and he was always so strict, but after all the trouble we sang real well."

"Do your children sing too?"

"Oh, yes," exclaimed the spokesman.

"Keep quiet when other people are talking."

"But my sister, sir, sings out of tune!"

"Sister?" The curate looked round at the little girls.

"Oh, no, not any of these."

"Have you a sister somewhere else?"

"Sure—Lena, of course."

"Then you have more children, mother?"

"Yes, pastor, the oldest girl is away from home working. She is twelve years old."

"Oh, I tell you, she's so nice and grand and dressed up fine; if she would only come home so that we could see her pretty soon," said the spokesman.

"Where does she work?" asked the curate with a sudden presentiment.

"At Värnanäs, sir."

"Aha!" he exclaimed, "that's the face I was trying to remember. I knew I had seen it somewhere. Mother, I can greet you from your kind and beautiful daughter. It was because of the resemblance to her that I recognized you."

"What, sir?" The mother and her children looked at him with eyes sparkling and as much excitement as though expecting to hear the world's greatest news.

"Yes, I can greet you from her; I met her this morning at Värnanäs. I understand now, it must have been she. She looked like you, mother. Your daughter showed me the way, and I am under a certain obligation to her. Has she a good position at Värnanäs? Is she working for Mrs. Mannerskantz?"

"Oh, that's what you consider a good place!"

"Why so?"

"She is only a nurse girl for the manager of the estate. I think that's good enough for Lena. Thank Heaven, she has a nice place!"

"She's dear, fine, and grand!" cried two of the

oldest girls. "We saw her when she was home last. She gave each one of us a big penny, and that's worth a lot of fish, sir."

"Let me see if I haven't got a little remembrance with me from her," said the minister, and pulled out a narrow piece of white tape, about two feet long, from his vest pocket. "She dropped this in the path, while I was walking behind her, and I picked it up. I'll give that to you," he said to the largest of the girls.

Now the joy became rampant. "What a ribbon! What a nice ribbon! That's Sister Lena's! Lena's ribbon! Lena's ribbon!"

The children ran around, examined the narrow band, which had apparently been either a part of a child's waist or a baby's swaddling-cloth, and tried it on, now over their hair, now on their arms. In their eyes Sister Lena occupied such a high and glorious position that it seemed just as important and remarkable to hear from her as for the young ladies of a nobleman's family to get news from their sister, a countess or baroness, at the royal court.

The curate's thoughts were interrupted by the opening of the door, and in came the tall, gray-haired cantor. The fisherman's wife began to tremble, but a glance from the newcomer quieted her fear immediately. "Elin!" he said, "I see that you haven't set the table yet for the pastor, and since your husband Jonas, the jolly old soul, is still away and has the keys to the larder with him, so to speak, it is not surprising that you haven't prepared anything better. You have known me, though, from youth—and know full well—and now it would have been my humble wish and request," he continued with a bow to the preacher, "to have had Mother Elin, her family, and her distinguished guest take dinner with me to-day. But then I thought she wouldn't come to my house—which she very seldom does, and wouldn't let the children go up to the centre of the village for the same reason that they didn't go to church to-day—and I knew the pastor wouldn't come either without them —therefore I thought, if you would permit it, Mother Elin, I'd have Kersti bring over a few dishes of fish from my place, of our plain islander's food."

Mother Elin did not answer, but the expression in her face as she stared at the tall, hoary patriarch was exceedingly touching; in all probability she had looked that way when singing her hymns for him as a girl. He seemed a little ashamed and penitent in the presence of the clergyman, while his maid Kersti carried in one heaping dish after another of the islands' richest product. Sea fowl was not forgotten, nor good bread and fresh butter, and brandy was served in a large bottle of the latest seaman style from the nearest borough, Kristianopel.

The boisterous children suddenly became silent

and respectful at the sight of all these bounties, and crept into the corners of the room. One is always confused by anything unusual. In company with their daily guest, hunger, they had been intimate, cheerful, impetuous; now, before all this food, they stood bewildered and constrained.

"No, no, my dear Elin, don't bother," said the cantor in a friendly whisper to the woman who, in order to act as hostess in some particular, started to take out her two China plates and a glass; "just let them be and say nothing. Kersti has got all those things with her in a bundle. And let the youngsters come up to the table. This kind of parson likes that sort of thing. Just behave as if this were nothing extraordinary."

All began to eat, and the curate on his part also acted as though nothing had happened. For humanity's sake he would have preferred to see this charity practiced without his exhortation. But thank Heaven it turned out as well as it did!

When the meal was well under way, the patriarch of the skerries began to converse with his real guest, though always with a little timidity and fear. "It is an exceptionally great joy," he said, "and a wonderful grace of God," he continued, "when a fine young minister, whom we have never seen before, pays us a visit on this remote part of the coast. I have also been among people, though a poor man, and I've seen Kalmar in my day.

There's a fine cathedral in that city, pastor; only a rich man could have built such a church!"

"Yes, it is a beautiful and celebrated building," replied the curate, "a splendid memorial to Charles XI and his great architect, Tessin. With the exception of the Lund Cathedral, there is perhaps not a more magnificent temple in Sweden. It is a pleasure to see the wealthy use their riches to promote what is good and noble on earth; and they can show it much better and in other ways than by erecting buildings."

"I am of the opinion, sir," interrupted the cantor, "that the rich would readily do what was good and lovable if the ministers of the Gospel would only tell them to."

"But the well-to-do," interposed the curate, with a look at the cantor in answer to his private excuse, "who are Christians themselves ought to remember their duties toward their neighbors, even though the minister is not present, for he cannot be with them constantly."

"Eat, Mother Elin, and give Lars some more," urged the old man with a friendly glance at the disturbed woman and her bashful brood. "Eat, my dear children!"

"When you're getting old, it's a pleasure," continued the speaker, "to recall your boyhood. I was once as young as you, sir," he said with a tearful look at the curate; "I don't believe I was so hand-

some and light-haired, sir — still — pardon me if I
ask how old you are."

"Twenty-three."

"Great heavens! Twenty-three years — yes, that's
a pleasure. I also have been twenty-three. But the
old men who came to preach to us, while they spoke
like you in the church, sir, they did n't act like you
outside, and therefore — the cantor became what
he is and behaves as he did to-day, sir. Eat some
of the fowl, too, my dear Mother Elin. Your husband will surely be home very soon with the rest of
the crowd! This is good wild duck, don't you think?
Eat, Jakob, Sven —"

"Don't urge them so much, father; they have n't
had a good meal perhaps for several days. You
might make them sick now by your charity, as
before by —"

The old man interrupted suddenly, "Don't think
ill of us here on the coast, sir. I have never been
an enemy of poor people, even though I spoke
rather harshly to-day; but I did n't know you, sir;
I thought you would choose the kind of people
that everybody else does."

"Everybody else does? There is no minister who
is not the friend and protector of the poor."

"Don't say that, sir — pardon me — for when the
minister comes, he tries to get into the homes of the
highest and wealthiest, and he never sees the poor
man except to snub him and tell him to go to work

and earn his living. Just as if there were plenty
of work and money! Drink some of this, pastor!
Drink, Mother Elin! Therefore, you can understand, sir—since we always follow the example of
the better class—why we also are ashamed of the
poor, God help us, and don't like to have any one
go in and see how they live here on the islands."

"Let us say nothing more about the subject. I
hope your kindness will last, even after I am gone.
How does it happen that you have no wife and
children?"

"Children? Wife and children—wife and children—Eh, well, sir—they are dead, they—I am
ninety-one years old, Your Reverence—I was living in King Fredrik's time."

"So God has not blessed you with his greatest
gift?"

"Children, sir? That blessing costs money."

The young curate looked at the aged man at his
side with a certain feeling of repugnance. The cantor saw it, and said with rather a blank smile, "I
don't suppose you are married, pastor, are you?"

"No."

"Well, there you are. I suppose you'll want
about a dozen; young people always do."

"That matter is entirely in God's hands."

"Oh, yes, of course—yes, certainly."

"But—naturally—if one has naughty, wicked,
vicious children, then—"

"It's no blessing. No, certainly not."

"Still, I think—if you have a good, tender wife and you possess the same desirable qualities as she —the children, with the help of God, will seldom become wicked."

"A good wife, yes. Yes, certainly."

"To be sure, there are exceptions, and accidents may happen. Nevertheless, if those who marry love each other, I believe—"

"Your Reverence, a poor man must make a living, and he marries the richest girl he can get. On these rocky islands, among us poor wretches, it means simply that I—one marries the least poverty-stricken girl one can find."

"That's the principle you followed. I am not acquainted with your adventures, father, but such a method might not give you the kindest wife possible." .

"Well, she died forty years ago, and I am still living in the house I got with her. Now I have enough fish as long as I live. One can't ask anything more."

"Was that all the pleasure you received, cantor? Not even any children!"

"Children eat you out of house and home, sir. I had a son—a regular rascal. God have mercy on him; he died ten years ago."

"But did you notice these eight children, father? They had decorated the place to please their mother, and never said a word about food, when she came from church."

"Well, they 're not used to anything better, poor things."

"Your son was, though, as I understand. Is that the reason he was so self-willed?"

"One pleases the youngsters as long as one has the means. And yet, God knows — he was a scamp — alas!"

"That was the fellow who helped grandpa steal, sir," exclaimed the oldest lad, the spokesman.

The old man looked at him with a grim and frigid glance.

"Do you already know — boy?" he cried, but interrupted himself.

The curate became attentive at these words. Perhaps he thought this explained the old man's attitude toward the poor fisherman's family : "Grandpa" had led the cantor's son astray.

"Yes, my God!" exclaimed the mother, with a suppressed sigh. "If it had n't been for your son, Jan, my father would certainly not have been in jail now."

The cantor's fixed glances became gloomier and gloomier. "Yes, God have mercy on us, miserable wretches," he said.

The preacher shuddered. The evil influence had been in the other direction. It was Jan, the product of the patriarch's glorious economic calculations, who had led the grandfather astray.

"Console yourself, old, unfortunate man!" said the good-natured minister, turning toward the cantor. "If your son, as it appears, was the cause of the grandfather's crime and the sorrows of these people, you have a good opportunity now to help them like a neighbor, to make amends for all trouble, and obtain for yourself the greatest possible joy during your last days."

The old man stared at the preacher with a vacant and astonished look.

"Yes — plainly speaking — I mean you ought to take these children, feed them, and educate them."

"They have their own father, Jonas, sir."

"But I have heard that he went off several days ago, and some one saw his boat capsize. Perhaps he is —"

"Drowned, you mean. Yes, Jonas was always a wild bird on the open sea."

"Well, then, be the protector of the widow and her fatherless children. God has not for nothing left you without dependents."

The patriarch raised his tall head and looked wonderingly, first at the young, handsome clergyman by his side, then at Elin and her children. Apparently he intended to answer.

Just then a sudden noise struck their ears. The sound of oars was audible, and the cries along the whole shore rose louder and louder: "They 're coming! They're coming! They're here! They're here!"

"The fishing-fleet has arrived!"

"And your five richly laden boats," added the curate expressively.

But nobody listened to him now or answered his humanitarian suggestion.

The children rushed up to them. "Father's coming! Father's coming!" they yelled and dashed out. The rest rose from the table. The blessing after the meal was sudden and brief. "My five boats!" muttered the old man with a thoughtful calculating look, then took his stick and went out. Even the mother half forgot her guest in her joy at meeting her husband, who had been absent so long. She ran out of the cottage.

The curate went out also and decided to climb a hill a short distance away, where he could see and enjoy undisturbed the picturesque sight of a returning fishing party.

To the curate there were many new objects in the extensive, variegated picture before him. It swarmed with life. Everybody in the village, young and old, had streamed down to the shore, limping, hopping, puffing, laughing, cheering, and waving hats. Thirty boats, filled with sturdy, happy people, men and women, were approaching with quick strokes. The afternoon sun gilded the fishing tackle, and when the boats had finally made their way

through reeds and lithe sea-grass, the returning
fishermen stepped ashore, with the customary singing. The fish were taken from the nets and tackle,
and put in shining heaps on the ground, while the
whole scene took on the appearance of the gayest
fair, or rather of a family feast. Children joined their
parents, helped them sort, pile up, and count the
fish, rejoiced over the rich catch, cheered, com-
pared their amount with their neighbor's, made a
racket, and quarreled a little, and all had a fine time.

The visiting pastor was really curious to see the
celebrated Jonas, the husband of his hostess. Still
he remained at a distance watching everything and
observing the changes of the motley scene. Occasionally he caught a glimpse of his poor pets, the
widow's children, and their mother in the crowd.
Now and then he could hear a cry caused by too
violent jostling. Often the poorest dressed have to
give way.

Suddenly he heard a wild, terrible shriek followed by loud, prolonged wailings. Amazed, he
looked down and saw the eight children in line has-
tening away from the happy group. "He did n't
come! He'll never come back!" These words were
distinctly audible to the clergyman.

Their father? Then Jonas was lost.

Cruel sight! Joy was everywhere; poverty alone
was robbed of its last hope. The wealthy lost
nothing. Parents, relatives, and children arrived

with a fresh abundance. Now empty barrels were rolled down to the shore; soon the packing was to begin for shipment to Kalmar, Karlskrona, and perhaps even to Stockholm. Only the fatherless, in a grayish-brown, ragged, mournful procession, turned dismally aside to make way for the rolling casks. It was a miracle, too, that three of the youngest, especially the little fellow who had just learned to walk, were not crushed beneath the large kegs that rushed down the hill to enclose the day's harvest.

Where did the mother go? She had taken the smallest child on her arm to save it from being trampled to death under the feet of the jostling crowd. She went away with her children, afraid of the happiness that surrounded her on all sides, afraid of light, and harassed by the very rays of the sun. The curate's eyes followed her steps. He noticed her seeking a remote spot. She seemed like an exile from life. "Is there not a cloud in the sky to serve as a cover and protection from the burning sun? When sorrow passes over the earth, why should light mock its poverty with joyous rays! But I must not go on like this," exclaimed the curate, interrupting his fantastic monologue. "I still hope to find aid," he said, when he saw the last dark gray rag disappear behind a slender, beautiful young birch. "I don't know where they are going now, but I will not let the patriarchal cantor get out of my sight. He must become a new father to them in place of him who was drowned."

The curate directed his attention again toward the crowd. The activity had increased, and the Sabbath was entirely forgotten. Soon he discovered a towering, commanding figure, a head taller than the rest; everything about him that smacked of hymns and church duties had now been completely discarded. The greedy fisherman chief stood among his subordinates and neighbors like a little idol. The preacher looked at him with a feeling akin to disgust. There was no doubt that this man, who in church was the all-powerful leader in the hymns, was now also the centre and director of the other village affairs, including the management of the fishing. The grim and eager counting, the sorting of the fish, the struggling with nets, traps, boat-hooks, and all kinds of apparatus — the sharp and harsh voice audible above the clamor of a hundred others — the good supply of bizarre oaths characteristic of the skerries — all this was quite discouraging to the young minister's hope of assistance for his hiding friends.

The curate began to figure out his own prospective income, and concluded that he could probably provide a temporary relief, but how about a more permanent support? Impossible! He did not know yet the nature of his own pastor's personal charities. He knew from custom that the mother

parish would take great precautions to keep the
poor of the adjacent territory outside her own district, and there were no prospects of a poorhouse
for the residents of the chapelry.

With these thoughts he started off, following
the direction taken by the eight children and their
mother when they disappeared from the scene. He
walked quietly, advancing between the trees which
here formed a little enclosure. After a time, he
heard the sound of words, in the distance, faint but
melodious, resembling an address. He came nearer
undetected. He could hear the woman repeat several of the expressions that he himself had used in
the morning.

"What is this?" he thought.

There sat the mother on a high stone, with her
whole little congregation gathered around her on
the grass, giving the substance of the sermon which
she, but not they, had heard that morning. The
listening minister could not help feeling that her
words were very much better chosen than his own.
They were much more fervent, milder, better suited
for exhortation, and directed more to the audience.
Moreover, the attention of this little group was
absolutely perfect. She spoke of another father for
them: a heavenly father. "Now let us be happy,"
she said with a comforting countenance. Just then,
however, a flood of tears burst forth and rolled
down her cheeks. The children sobbed quietly, not

loudly and offensively. They sat in a grove so far away that the noise made by the more fortunate in the village did not trouble or wound them. After the mother had recovered, she began to sing a melody not unlike a cradle song, probably composed by herself, for the words pictured her bridal procession, how at fifteen she had danced the merry bridal dance; and she added a new verse for each successive year, that is, for each one of her children. Jonas, too, the mighty "islander," was described in the refrain of every verse.

This little service seemed like an evening song to the curate. He finally emerged from his hiding-place. The children gave a loud cry of joy; he had already become their friend. He sat down on a knoll beside them and began to dispel their sorrow by fairy tales. He himself was a man who still loved the lovable, being only twenty-three years old.

With the mother he discussed a plan for their future. "My only hope, next to God, is my oldest daughter," she said. "Though she is only twelve years old, Lena is an intelligent child. She has a good place, she will help her younger brothers and sisters to get something too."

"A nurse girl? And working for an overseer only? What a support!" thought the curate. It occurred to him to go to Värnanäs and personally try his luck with Mrs. Mahnerskantz. Yet he hesitated when he remembered the bad reputation of islanders on the mainland. He pictured in his mind the head he had seen near the curtain in the morning, and wondered whether he could associate it with charity.

"I shall leave here very soon," he concluded. "The sun has gone down. The time is passing. But I shall not forget you."

"Dear pastor," replied Mother Elin, "I can stand the grief quite well to-day. Fresh wounds give no pain. It'll be worse to-morrow, and still worse the next day. If I only had his body! But the sea is greedy, and the waves are hungry."

"The Son of God will comfort you."

"The eye will become dry in time," she said, "and folded hands will be separated. Still sorrow will remain in the heart, and agony is the food of the fatherless."

He did not venture any further reply. He saw a dark, gloomy circle around her shining eyes. She appeared scarcely to notice her immediate surroundings.

She continued, "The seal barks on the ice, his parent hears him and comes to him. The otter has a friend, and the sea-serpent does not open his jaws for seaweed in vain. So my children have me— but I have nothing for them. When the sea-eagle plunges down he catches pickerel in his claws and carries them home to his unfeathered brood. Little Anna is unfeathered, Sven is unfeathered, and

Matts has no clothes. Jakob and Kersti, where is your sea-eagle — who was to bring home pickerel to you? I will tell you where the eagle is. He dug his claws into a big, strong fish, which pulled him down beneath the water. Oh — o-oh! I can see how he struggled with wings and beak — way down — down — down he had to go — had to go — and it was dark — so dark for him down in the deep!"

At the end of these words, which the unhappy woman had spoken with the expression of a visionary, she sank down overcome with terror near the tree where she had been sitting. The confused children gazed at her with staring eyes, and were silent from sheer fright.

After a short time she got up with clear eyes, and appeared to be listening intently. "What's that? What do I hear?" she exclaimed. "Jonas, that's your own song I hear!"

The clergyman, who heard nothing, believed the poor woman was delirious. She sat down calmly on a stone, her eyes were fixed on the grass without really looking at anything; she seemed all ears. "It's he! Jonas!" she cried now and then, with convulsive movements. The oldest boy was listening sharply, like his mother. The curate heard nothing. "It comes from the north!" said the lad.

"A merry song, I recognize it!" she cried suddenly during an interval, starting up, but sitting down again, silent as death.

The minister was amazed. He remembered that these children of nature are reputed to have an extraordinary sense both of hearing and of sight. He looked northward over the sea, but a point of land blocked the view. Finally he also heard a tone like the whistling of the gay summer wind.

"It's coming nearer," she said, and sprang up. Beside herself, she lifted the youngest child high in the air as if for public exhibition, kissed it, set it again on the grass, and hurried down to the shore. From there one had a magnificent view over the bay, now illumined by the evening sun's most friendly rays. The curate followed the mother. At that moment the bow of a boat swung around the cape to the north, and then another, and still another.

The woman cried, "That's the north fishing-fleet returning! Do you see Jonas? He's the steersman of the first boat. You'll see, he will land here. I knew he didn't like the south-bound crowd."

With lively strokes the approaching mariners cleft the seaweed and came ashore to the following song:

> Come, row the vessel home
> From where the billows roam,
> Across the shining foam!
> Come, heave ashore, lads,
> The whitefish, pike, and perch, the bream and salmon fair,
> And spread them on the grass as golden treasures rare.
> And then good store, lads,

Of sturgeon, carp, sardines, and eels and other fishes,
Oh, lay them on the good greensward like piles of silver dishes.
> *King of the sea,—*
> *Such, young or old, should the fisherman be.*
> *When he sails away,*
> *He's thrall to the storm,*
> *Every day.*
> *But when with his heap*
> *Of spoil from the deep*
> *He turns his back*
> *Past the skerries black,*
> *Sweet memories often*
> *His spirit will soften—*
> *Love and singing and dancing he seeks him*
> *On land.*
> *When he's won his spoil*
> *From the dark waves' moil*
> *He will gaily fare*
> *With his dear-bought share*
> *To a fragrant meadow*
> *That boughs overshadow—*
> *Love and singing and dancing he seeks then.**

While repeating once more the last part of his "barcarole" a tall man jumped ashore. Scarcely had he seen Elin, when he took her in his arms, paying no attention whatever to the clergyman, and he came near throwing her up in the air just as she had done immediately before with their youngest child. He was a type of genuine sailor, and the exact,

* Verse translated by Charles Wharton Stork.

enlarged image of the boy whom we have called
the spokesman. His face was lean and angular, with
a lively, almost reckless expression, and his long,
flying hair was covered by a threadbare hat of ludi-
crous shape.

"Now we are rich, Elin!" he cried; "do you
see?"

"What kind of crew are you bringing, Jonas?"

"Friends and old sailors, every one of them,
whom I hired to take home my boats, and who
afterwards will go to—"

"And you did n't get drowned, as they said?"

"Oh, I went down all right, and my boat was
lost. But I came up again, you see, and some good
people coming along took me in their tender. But
heigh-ho!—that has nothing to do with this. Understand, I own these boats here, all of them loaded
to the limit. And now I 'll build a house in the village, a great, big one! Even bigger than that old
devil's—"

"The cantor's," said the curate to himself.

"And then we 'll get grandpa out of jail!" cried
the boy spokesman.

"Yes, indeed."

"Tell me, though, Jonas," asked his wife seriously, "how did you become so rich?"

"I am a good pilot, you see; there is n't a better
one on Kalmar Bay, or on the whole Kalmar Sound.
Well, a foreign vessel, with an English captain,

had ventured north of Klippan, between Öland and us, and he did n't know the channels. His crew had pulled me into their tender, when I was swimming and splashing in the water, and taken me to his ship. All of a sudden, after sailing a short distance, he ran aground so hard that if it had n't been for Jonas, I'm afraid—Well—we worked hard all night, and when I had finally repaired all the damage—oh, he was a fine fellow—he gave me a handful of English money. No pilot ever got so much, though no pilot, except God, ever did what Jonas did that night. Since I knew that nobody understood such money in the skerries, I went to Kalmar, to Mr. Näv, to have it exchanged. I told my story and became a big man in the whole town. Then I bought these boats—hey, Elin, there's going to be some fishing now!—and a lot of cloth, mutton, cognac, and fine bread. Carry things ashore, my friends, and get them ready! We are going to have refreshments at once, right here on the grass—This is my wife, good and beautiful—three years younger than Jonas himself—and here are eight little urchins: not one of you, boys, has as many as that—one does n't get them on the sea. And if you want to visit me next year about this time, you'll see my new house, as big as the town hall—one has to have something for such a big family, says old man Nordenankar. But who is that gentleman there? Oh, our new pastor, I presume!

Well, I 'm a regular sea-gull, sir; you 'll have to pardon me. I should have kept still; maybe you, pastor, talked this morning to these people out here, and maybe to Elin, too. So, I have to talk now at nightfall, for each one has his own time to preach, as they say in Kalmar."

Just then another boat came round the point. "Look, there 's my fourth," cried Jonas; "she 's a little slow, not so swift as the other three, and yet she carries my most valuable cargo." Mother Elin gazed at the approaching skiff with wide open eyes; she thought her husband rich enough already. The curate also looked in the same direction. The sturdy rowers put ashore, and a girl of eleven or twelve jumped out.

"Yes, Elin," said Jonas, "you mustn't wonder why I stayed away so long, for I have got together a good many things, and done quite a lot. Last of all I stopped at Värnanäs, as you see; I was there a couple of hours ago and visited the Manner-skantz family. Between you and me—I brought back to them a very good friend who had been aboard that English ship I told you about, and who would have gone to the bottom, with every-thing else, if it had n't been for the Lord and Jonas. Well, you can understand why I was so welcome at Värnanäs, though an islander. The face of one person in particular soon got its color back at seeing this dear friend, who had returned as though from the jaws of death. Now, you know, Elin, the better class think they can't show gratitude toward us in any way except by money — so, being a shore-dweller, I took what was offered — and that's all right. You'll see they gave me quite a sum. Then I went down to the overseer's to find out how Helena was, and when I saw her sitting there, rocking the cradle and singing, it made me feel happy. I kissed her, and I happened to think that I too wanted my child at home. I spoke to the overseer and, although he did n't like to have her go, we finally came to an agreement. So I took my Helena along down to the boats, and here she is, as you see. She's named after you, mother, and in time she'll be just as pretty and good as you."

The beautiful scene of the reunion — the happiness of the children — the fresh color that appeared on fair Helena's pale cheeks at the return to her home — the mother's pride at the sight of such a large family which she could now feed and clothe — the young clergyman's delight —

But wait: this narrative occupies only one day, Sunday, and it is now almost six o'clock, when the Sabbath ends.

The kind, benevolent minister took his farewell, left the chapel, and made his way to the mother church and the residence of the rector.

If the story did not end here, much could be told which happened later. It should be mentioned

how the preacher of the chapel, whose illness had
led to the unexpected sermon of the day, died a
short time afterwards, and how the popular young
curate became his successor, first as substitute during the year of grace, and then as regular chaplain. It might be told how the magnate, the cantor,
also departed this life the day after information had
come from Karlskrona that the imprisoned grandfather, weighed down by toil and age, had ended
his days beside an anchor-bill in one of the anchor
shops. The problem of his release from prison, so
much desired by his grandchildren — had such a
release been permitted by law — was therefore settled for them. It should be described also how the
active and sturdy Jonas built his new house, and
soon became through deed and counsel his neighbors' foremost guide, friend, and leader, both in
the fishing vocation and in other conditions of life.
It ought to be pictured further how the energy of
the new chaplain reformed the skerries into a home
of peace and love, and how he confirmed Helena
at the age of fifteen. She was eleven or twelve years
younger than he, but is that such a big difference?

Years came and went, but the chaplain would
never move from his little place. He had allied
himself too closely with the parishioners. Born of
peasant parents, he found his happiness in a circle
of good, sensible, and industrious country people,
who were ennobled through his prayers and holy

care. When the minister of a congregation agrees with and solicits the advice of its best and most prominent member—as was the case with the chaplain and his father-in-law, the mighty fisherman, Jonas—it will almost always turn out well. The skerries, often rough, scraggy, barren, and terrible to behold, enjoy in many of their concealed coves a mild balmy wind, and the summer smiles a long time behind the shelter of the cliffs.

THE END

PUBLICATIONS OF

THE AMERICAN–SCANDINAVIAN FOUNDATION

Committee on Publications

SCANDINAVIAN CLASSICS

I. *Comedies by Holberg: Jeppe of the Hill, The Political Tinker, Erasmus Montanus.*
Translated by OSCAR JAMES CAMPBELL, JR., and FREDERIC SCHENCK.

II. *Poems by Tegnér: The Children of the Lord's Supper* and *Frithiof's Saga.*
Translated by HENRY WADSWORTH LONGFELLOW and W. LEWERY BLACKLEY.

III. *Poems and Songs by Björnstjerne Björnson.*
Translated in the original metres, with an Introduction and Notes, by ARTHUR HUBBELL PALMER.

IV. *Master Olof by August Strindberg.*
Translated, with an Introduction, by EDWIN BJÖRKMAN.

V. *The Prose Edda by Snorri Sturluson.*
Translated from old Icelandic, with an Introduction and Notes, by ARTHUR GILCHRIST BRODEUR.

Made in the USA
Lexington, KY
04 October 2010